I started down the dimly lit walk to the street, hearing my own steps slapping the pavement. Suddenly, I heard another sound, someone moving behind me. A shiver ran down my back. A minute ago, when I'd left the library, there'd been no one around; the parking lot was empty. If someone had left after me—a librarian—she or he would be driving! Who else would be here this time of night? Michael? No. He'd left half an hour ago!

I quickened my step and glanced back to see a dark figure hurrying toward me. Run, my head commanded. Run! Get to where people driving might see you if someone tries to attack! Perspiration ran down my neck. My heart pumped off the scale. Why hadn't I listened to Mrs. Cohen? Oh God, I prayed, *Save me!*

DESPERATE PURSUIT

Gloria D. Miklowitz

BANTAM BOOKS
NEW YORK • TORONTO • LONDON • SYDNEY • AUCKLAND

RL 6, age 12 and up

DESPERATE PURSUIT

A Bantam Book/May 1992

The Starfire logo is a registered trademark of Bantam Books, a division of Bantam Doubleday Dell Publishing Group, Inc. Registered in U.S. Patent and Trademark Office and elsewhere.

ISBN 0-553-29746-5

Published simultaneously in the United States and Canada

Bantam Books are published by Bantam Books, a division of Bantam Doubleday Dell Publishing Group, Inc. Its trademark, consisting of the words "Bantam Books" and the portrayal of a rooster, is Registered in U.S. Patent and Trademark Office and in other countries. Marca Registrada. Bantam Books, 666 Fifth Avenue, New York, New York 10103.

PRINTED IN THE UNITED STATES OF AMERICA

RAD   0   9   8   7   6   5   4   3   2

DESPERATE PURSUIT

CHAPTER 1

"I'LL BE DONE around four-thirty," Michael told me the day I met Shane, the day my whole life changed.

We'd just come from lunch and Michael had walked me to English class. "I'm playing this new guy, supposed to have a wicked backhand, but we shouldn't go past four-thirty. Meet me at the courts and we'll go for something to eat after, okay?" he added.

He always planned ahead like that. He wanted me to know where he'd be, wanted to know where I'd be at any given moment. It made me feel secure, because it meant he really cared. "You'll clobber him in two sets, knowing you," I said with confidence.

A small, doubting scowl darkened Michael's face. "Oh, I don't know. I don't think so . . ."

"Hear ye! Hear ye!" I pretended to talk through a

megaphone. "This is Nicole speaking! Michael Donaldson is a winner, regardless of what his father says!"

Michael's face lit up and he stood straighter.

It was no secret how I felt about Michael's dad. Mr. Donaldson probably did love his sons, but he always gave them a hard time. The first time I realized how impossible he was was at the state tennis tournament. I sat beside Mr. Donaldson the whole time, and no matter how well Michael played, he always found fault. Michael had trained hard and played well and he deserved praise. Statewide he'd captured second place.

You'd have thought Mr. Donaldson would have been ecstatic. No way. He was as grim as an undertaker. When we pushed through the crowds and found Michael after the game, Michael let out a joyous yell and waved the trophy high over his head.

"You were terrific!" I exclaimed, flinging my arms around him. "I'm so proud of you!"

He hugged me hard and grinned, then his gaze shifted. "Dad? What did you think?"

"Why'd you let Larsen take you in the second set?" Mr. Donaldson asked. "How come you didn't play net like I told you?"

"I . . . I . . ." Michael tried, the pleasure in his win already spoiled. "Well, you see . . ."

It broke my heart to hear him sputtering apologies when he should have been basking in well-earned praise. I couldn't stand it after a while. Trying hard to sound respectful I said, "Michael's the best tennis player the school has had in fifteen years, Mr. Donaldson! He played the best he could! He *took* second place!"

"Young lady," Mr. Donaldson returned, "in our family, we only settle for the best. There's only one *best*. That's *first*. Michael knows that! So does his brother!"

Now, as Michael turned away, tall and trim in white tennis shirt and shorts, I thought again how lucky I was that he'd started dating me. I was younger, but he didn't care. Everyone liked him, even my parents.

We'd met last year, at a party when I was a freshman. I was ecstatic that a junior wanted to be with me. His crowd was great, and they made me feel welcome. I'd been going with Michael ever since. I'd never had a boyfriend before. Everything was new and exciting. All the girls said I was so lucky. Michael had absolutely no interest in anyone else once we met. He treated me like a princess. He drove me to school, to the mall, anywhere I wanted. He didn't care if my best friend, Evie, came along sometimes, either. He bought me little presents, sent me flowers, and bought me a heart necklace for my birthday. We went to all of his friends' dances and parties. Sometimes I did feel a little overwhelmed, though.

"Michael," I begged once, "I like to stay home now and then and just read a book. Or . . . something. . . ." I added, meekly, when I saw the look on his face.

"Do I stop you from doing anything? Do I? That hurts, Nicole. You want to read some night, fine. I'll bring a book over and read with you. You're the best thing that has ever happened to me. Every minute I'm with you makes me happy."

That wasn't what I meant, but I figured that must be how boyfriends act when they really like you.

Evie said, "Michael *loves* you, that's all. It's a compliment that he wants to be with you all the time! I should be so lucky!"

"You?" I exclaimed in surprise. Evie always went for the wounded-bird shy guy. The one who couldn't make friends, or who got in trouble. "Michael's not your type, Evie! He's got his act together!" She'd thrown me an embarrassed grin.

Evie was right, I realized. Michael loved me. He'd said so, more than once, and it made me feel so *good*. But I'd also get a little squirmy, because I couldn't honestly say I loved him back. I *liked* Michael, a lot. He was good company and always there for me. But there was something missing. I couldn't even say what, because I'd never been out with anyone else. I wanted to love him, told myself I should, but I knew down deep that I didn't. Whenever he got on the subject of love, I made a joke or changed the subject.

And that's the way things stood with us that day—before I met Shane.

At four o'clock I left the school library with Evie and meandered over to the tennis courts. It was a typical hot, sunny January day for California. Blue-blue skies and a desert wind to dry you off. Some of the nicest weather comes right after the new year—between rains.

The six courts behind the high school were all busy with tennis team practice. Michael and the guy he was playing were on a court near the street. Evie and I plunked down on a bench outside the chain-link fence to watch.

"Did he ask you to the prom yet?" Evie asked, pulling an orange from her pack. She bit into the skin to start the peel and a geyser of juice shot out. She looked great, as usual. Her dark, shiny hair hung in a thick braid down her back, and her clothes hung on her as if she were posing for a fashion magazine.

Mom said she had "good bones," whatever that means. I'd always wanted to look like Evie. Instead, my hair always curled when I wanted it to lay straight, and at five-four my bones were definitely "average."

Had Michael asked me to the prom? "Not yet," I said, waving to Michael when he glanced our way. "It's only January!"

"He will."

Across the net the guy Michael played swayed slightly right and left, legs apart, bent at the waist, racket poised.

Michael tossed the ball several times to get the feel of it then threw it high. He rose to his toes and brought his racket down with a hard *thwap*. The ball zinged across the net, hit the ground low, and flew off to stick in the chain-link fence just feet from where we sat.

"Way to go!" I clapped my hands and smiled with glee, just as Michael's opponent trotted up to the fence.

"Hello," he called, prying the ball out of the links.

"Hi!" I answered automatically. He was as tall as Michael, but not nearly as good-looking. He had a head of thick, reddish-brown hair, the bluest eyes I'd ever seen, and a funny little shy smile. We only traded glances for a second before he turned and jogged back to position on the court. But in that second I think I stopped breathing and a tingling started in my arms and legs.

"I *know* him!" Evie announced, passing me half of the orange. "He's new. From Texas or Florida or something. Name's funny. Shane, I think. Yeah—Shane."

"Shane. . . ." I took a deep breath.

"Match point!" Michael called, and I turned to watch him rise to his toes again for what would surely be the final serve, the final play. But it wasn't. Shane took the point and it was back to deuce. That's how it went for the next ten minutes, from match point to deuce, again and again.

I began to pay attention to Shane. He was good. Very good. But Michael was better. He had that killer instinct his father said every winner must have. He gave the game every ounce of concentration, lips drawn tight, forehead beaded with sweat. I heard the quiet grunt of exertion every time he served. He'd reach for impossible balls and lob them over the net or slam them into a corner. It was that extra determination that made the difference, finally. He beat Shane four sets to two.

"Sorry we took so long," Michael said as he trotted up to us, toweling his face and neck. "Man, it's nearly five." He stuck a hand out to Shane. "Didn't think you'd last so long. Good game. Thanks."

"Thanks to you! Any time," Shane said.

"We're going for some food, soon as I shower. Want to join us?" Michael asked.

"Sure. Thanks."

I couldn't understand why I felt so hot suddenly, and why I avoided looking at Shane. "You were terrific, Michael! Wasn't he, Evie?" I exclaimed, sounding like an idiot but unable to shut up.

Michael put an arm around me and grinned. "You always think I'm terrific. Oh, sorry. Forgot to introduce you. This is Shane. Shane, meet Evie and Nicole."

"Michael sure gave me a workout," Shane said, talking directly to me. "I always play best when my opponent is better than I am."

"Ahh . . ." Michael stammered, "I'm not so hot. Really." He studied his sneakers.

"Well, let's go, Evie!" I said brightly. "Give these guys a chance to shower. See you in the parking lot, ten minutes, guys." I strode away as fast as I could go.

"Hey, Nicole! *Wait up!*" Evie called, catching up to me. "My goodness, you're practically running! What's the hurry?"

I slowed down. "Don't know. I feel hot and cold all over, suddenly. Maybe I'm sick."

"Oh, poo! You're not sick. It's that Shane. I saw how you looked at him!"

"Evie!" I barked. "That's ridiculous!"

"Is it?" She laughed.

She was right, of course. It *was* Shane. From that day on nothing was ever the same.

CHAPTER
2

"HOW'D YOU GET the name Shane?" I asked, as we sat over drinks at the drive-in. We'd settled at an outside table, Shane and Evie on one side, Michael and I opposite. Shane had just explained that he'd moved to California from Texas, that his father had lost his job in the oil industry slump and was working now as an engineer. I told him that my father was an engineer, too, in aerospace.

He smiled at me over a big chocolate shake. "You won't believe this, but . . . all the kids in my family are named after movies. Mom loved the film *Shane*, so that's what I got. I've a sister called *Sabrina*." He paused, and then added, "And my kid brother is— don't laugh—*E.T.*"

"No!" We all looked at one another, then burst out laughing.

"Just kidding." His very-blue eyes steadied on me, and my face grew hot.

"Nice guy," Michael said later. "Good tennis player, too."

"Umm," I agreed, as if I didn't much care.

The next time I saw Shane was at the library, where I work three nights a week as a page. Lots of kids come evenings to study or fool around, so it's not unusual to see someone you know. I'd just shelved some books in the biography section when something caught my eye. There was Shane at a table in the back where the real students go, bent over a book.

I felt all fluttery inside and annoyed that my legs felt so unsteady. I didn't know if I believed in love at first sight. Michael had it for me. Did I have it for Shane?

I shelved more books, keeping an eye on him as I moved, but he never looked up. Finally, when I got close to his table I came up behind and whispered, "Hello, Texas."

His head swiveled around, and as he recognized me he grinned. "Hello, Imp."

I liked that image. Imp conjured up someone cute and mischievous. I blushed. "Homework?"

He closed the book on his finger. I saw the title. *Writer's Market.* This time *his* face flushed. "Just browsing. I'm a wanna-be writer. Short stories and little things like that. I'm not good enough to be published, but maybe someday."

I came around to perch for a moment on the chair near him. "What kind of stories do you write?"

"Science fiction, fantasy. . . ."

"I like fantasy. Maybe you could let me read something of yours sometime?"

"Sometime." He closed the book. "You work here?"

"Only three evenings a week and sometimes on Saturdays." I saw the librarian watching me. "I better get back or I'll be out of a job." I rose and pushed the book cart forward. "Bye, Texas. See you."

"Bye, Imp." He went back to his book, and left soon after.

When Michael arrived to drive me home after the library closed I felt a little guilty, but I didn't say a word about Shane.

"Telephone!" Mom called a few days later, while Michael was at the house. "Nicole! For you!"

I got up from the floor where Michael and I sat listening to a new musical group his dad's record company was promoting. "Probably Evie. Be right back," I said, going off to the phone.

"Hello?" the voice asked. "Nicole?"

Oh my! Shane! I clutched the receiver so hard it hurt.

"It's me—Texas," he said in a teasing way. "You know, the guy in the library?"

"I know. I recognize the accent."

"Aw shucks. I thought it didn't show."

I giggled.

"I wondered if you'd like to go out with me Saturday night. Got a job now. Be done at six, so I could pick you up around seven."

Yes! I wanted to shout. *Oh, yes! Yes!* But then I suddenly thought, Wait! How can you? What about Michael?

"We could go to a movie, or just talk. . . ." he added, in a lighthearted tone.

"I . . . I . . ." I stammered.

"Are you free? What do you say?"

"I . . . I don't know." I realized how peculiar that must sound, how unenthusiastic. Yet, I really didn't know. I always spent Saturday nights with Michael. He didn't even ask anymore; it was expected. Did that mean I could never date anyone else?

"*I don't know.* Now, how do I read that?" Shane chided. "Does it mean you have to check your calendar? Or does it mean you have to think about it? I don't want to be pushy, but I thought . . . I mean, I felt . . . you liked me."

"I do! I do!" I exclaimed, then lowered my voice. "I'd love to go out with you, Shane, except . . . I'm seeing Michael."

"Oh." For a second I thought he understood. After all, he'd seen the two of us together all the time. But then he asked, "How about next week, then?"

"You don't understand. Michael and I are going together."

"Oh, oh. . . . You don't ever date anyone else?"

"I haven't. . . ."

"Well, I guess that's that, then." His voice lost its playfulness. "Michael's one lucky guy."

"Thanks."

"Well . . . guess I'll see you at school."

"Wait!" I cried, afraid he'd hang up. "I do want to go out with you, Shane. I'd love to. It's okay! The Saturday after this will be fine!" My stomach knotted in sudden anxiety. What was I doing?

"And Michael?"

"It's okay. He'll understand."

"That's great! I'm really glad! I can hardly wait!"

I grinned at the phone. "Me too. Listen, I can't talk now. A—friend's here."

"I understand. See you at school! Bye!"

I hung up and wrapped my arms around myself, eyes closed. Shane liked me! He'd asked me out! Yeow!

"Nicole!" Michael called from the other room. "Hurry up! You're missing all the good stuff! Come on!"

I took a deep breath and tried to think stern thoughts to hide the smile I felt. Then I went back to the family room.

"What's up?" Michael asked. "You look funny. Who *was* that?"

I busied myself looking through the tapes. "Just a friend."

"Not Evie?"

I wanted to keep Shane's call my secret for a while. I dropped to the floor beside Michael and smiled. "Why don't you play that recording over so I can hear it? Come on, Michael. I heard some of it. Sounded great!"

"What do you mean, you want to date others?" Michael demanded, when I finally got up the courage to tell him. It was the next day. We were driving home from the library. I'd rehearsed what I'd say a zillion times and finally just spilled it out in the dark of the car so he couldn't see my face.

"What are you saying?" He gripped the steering wheel and darted quick looks in my direction. "You can't do that! We're going steady!"

"Michael," I said, turning to face him in the dim light. "Listen to me. I'm only fifteen. You're the first boy I ever went out with. I want to see what it's like." He scowled, so I added, "You know I like you . . . a lot!"

"*Like* me?"

"Evie says half the girls at school are crazy about you! You could get a date for next Saturday so easily! Just one phone call!"

Michael pulled to the curb in front of my house. He swung around. "I don't want another date. This isn't right. You can't do this, Nicole. I won't have it!"

"Oh, come *on*, Michael," I said, hearing a quaver in my voice. He sounded so angry, and I'd never stood up to him before. "It's one date! That's all! I may never want to see this guy again!"

"Who is *this* guy? Do I know him?"

When I didn't answer, he said, "I don't believe this. You're not leveling with me. You wouldn't risk our relationship if he wasn't important. Who is he? I'll straighten *him* out!" He grabbed my arm and squeezed hard. "Who, Nicole? Clark? Justin? Is it Matt? Tell me!"

"No!"

"Tell me!"

"Michael! You're hurting me!"

He loosened his grip. I almost gave in because his anger scared me, but then he seemed to collapse. He stared down at his hands and, in the softest, saddest voice, said, "I'm sorry. Nicole, I didn't mean to hurt you! I'd never do that. It's just that I don't understand. We have such a good thing going. What do you want? I'd do anything for you!"

I rubbed my arm and didn't answer.

"Don't do this, Nicole, please. Don't."

I took Michael's cold hands in mine, looked into his pleading eyes, and felt awful. He'd told me so often that I was the only good thing in his life, the only one who truly believed in him. Michael needed me. How could I hurt him like this?

But then he said, "I won't ask again, Nicole. We'll forget all about it. Just call this guy right now and tell him you're not going. Okay? Promise, Nicole!"

Something stubborn rose up in me. Usually, it takes a while for me to react to a hurt or an insult. I replay the words in my head hours after I've heard them and wish I'd stood up to the person. This time Michael's commanding words and tone struck me instantly. Who did he think he was? My father? My boss?

I dropped his hands. "No, I won't promise. I'm going to keep the date. I'm sorry. I don't want to hurt you, but that's what I want!"

Michael seemed astounded. "What about us?"

"For heaven's sake! What *about* us? All I'm doing is having one date. We'll still go out together. Unless you don't want to. . . ." I added as an afterthought.

"Of course I want to!"

"Then what's the fuss?" I smiled, but it was forced, and I felt a funny twinge of guilt. One date would never be enough. I already knew I'd want to see Shane again. And again. And at that moment I just didn't care if Michael liked it or not.

He must have picked up on my mood because he grumbled something, not satisfied, but then let it go.

I opened the car door and started out. Then, wanting to make things right between us, said, "Come in for a snack?"

"No thanks, not tonight."

I glanced back. Michael sat gripping the steering wheel and staring straight ahead. It tore at my heart, but I checked myself. He wanted me to feel guilty, to soothe his hurt feelings, to back down. Not this time! "Okay, Michael," I said. "See you tomorrow."

CHAPTER
3

I CAN'T UNDERSTAND how my feelings could change so fast and so completely, but they did. One day, Michael was the center of my life. I was proud to be his girlfriend and to spend so much time with him. The next—I wished he'd disappear. All of a sudden he seemed so constantly needy, so annoyingly bossy and demanding.

"Do you *have* to walk me to every class?" I asked irritably the next day. We had just passed Shane in the hall. I felt as if an electric current shot from me to him, and that Michael could feel it. Shane smiled and said, "Hi." It seemed as if he wanted to stop, but Michael just nodded and moved on, his hand at my back.

"I thought you *liked* me to walk you to class!" Michael said, surprised at my outburst.

"It's just that . . ." I softened at his hurt look. "It's

just that—sometimes I feel like you're guarding me, like you're trying to keep me away from everyone else."

"That's silly, Nicole! I walk you to class because I love being with you. And as for keeping you from others, didn't I introduce you to all my friends? Don't we always have lunch with the guys? How am I keeping you from other people?"

"Well"—I shrugged; the air had gone out of my argument—"sometimes I feel that way, just the same."

We arrived at my English class and Michael backed me against the wall, talking about the party we were going to Saturday night. There'd be lots of kids, a hundred maybe, and everyone had to bring something—pretzels or drinks or a dip. "I'll make an onion dip," I offered, as students milled around us.

My heart turned over. Across the hall I glimpsed Shane drinking from the water fountain. Was he hanging around, waiting for Michael to leave so we could talk? "You better go, Michael," I said. "You'll be late for history."

"What's the hurry? The first bell hasn't even rung yet. Trying to get rid of me?" He sounded irritated. "What about this afternoon? Where will you be so I can reach you?"

"That's just what I mean, Michael! Do I have to account for every minute I'm not in your company?"

"Down boy!" He backed off in mock terror and good-naturedly added, "Goodness! Aren't you the tiger!"

"I'm going to the mall with Evie," I said.

"If you wait until after tennis practice, I'll drive you."

"We can take the bus." I scooted out from under the arm caging me against the wall. "Gotta go in now, Michael. We're having a test."

"Okay. See you around eight. Oh! And good luck on the test."

"Thanks." I looked beyond Michael to the water fountain. Shane had gone. Disappointed, I went into the classroom.

The party Saturday night was so big that kids showed up who weren't even invited, and the whole house swarmed and vibrated until the police arrived because neighbors complained of the noise. It wasn't one of my favorite ways to spend an evening.

We got there around nine, left my onion dip on the dining room table, then poked around looking for kids we knew. We soon found a cluster of Michael's friends, and they got into a hot and noisy discussion about class elections. After a while I wandered off, bored. Maybe I'd find Evie and her date. She was seeing a junior now. Maybe—*maybe*—Shane heard about the party and came.

I peeked into a big recreation room at the end of the house where a lot of the kids were dancing, but didn't see either Shane or Evie. Disappointed, and a little lost, I started back to Michael. Suddenly, someone came up behind me and grabbed me around the waist. "Hey, Nicole!" a voice shouted in my ear. "Let's dance!" It was Evan, one of Michael's friends.

We squeezed back into the rec room, and for the next ten minutes we had such a great time dancing I forgot all about Michael. The music was good, and I loved to dance.

And then, over Evan's shoulder, I saw Michael heading our way. He looked madder than I'd ever seen him, and suddenly all the fun drained away. "Hey, guy!" He laid a firm hand on Evan's shoulder. "Take a hike, pal. Nicole's with me."

"Hey, lay off! Take it easy!" Evan pried Michael's hand away and rubbed his shoulder. For a second I thought he'd take a swing at him.

"Yeah, well—*you* take it easy!" Michael took me firmly by the elbow and pulled me away.

"*Michael!* Quit it!" I cried, dragging to a stop in the hall and yanking free. "What's going on? You had no right! Evan saw me standing alone and asked me to dance. What's wrong with that? I can dance with whomever I want! You don't own me!"

"Is he the one who asked you out?" Michael demanded, not even caring what people could hear. "I bet he is!"

"You starting *that* again?"

He lowered his voice. "You're driving me nuts. I don't know what to think. What's happening to you? You're turning against me!"

"Stop that! I'm not turning against you!"

"What do *you* call it? I take you to a party and turn my back for one minute and where are you? Off somewhere without me, with another guy! Why don't you tell me who you're going out with?"

"No! It's not your business! You've got to stop this! You're smothering me!" I swung around and blindly pushed toward the door.

"Where are you going?" Michael leaped to my side. "Nicole! Slow down! Where are you going?"

"Home!"

"Please don't. I'm sorry. I didn't mean to upset you. It's just that you've got me suspecting every guy who looks twice at you. If you'd only tell me who it is, I could handle it."

I shook him off. "Leave me alone! I'm going home!"

"I'll take you."

"I can take myself."

"Nicole, cut it out! I brought you. I'll take you home." He shouldered his way through the crowd and finally we were outside and walking down the path to the street. We found his red Mustang and he unlocked the door. I swung by him and climbed in, crossed my arms, and stared straight ahead.

Michael climbed into the driver's seat and turned to me. "All right, I'm sorry. How many times do I have to say that? I acted like a creep, okay? But understand. Today was one rotten day. Dad's back from his trip to New York City. You know what it was like at dinner? A friggin' cross-examination! When I couldn't remember the name of the king of Saudi Arabia and Matt didn't know it either, he made us feel this big!" Michael held his thumb and forefinger a quarter inch apart. "And Mom just served the dinner and looked upset. I sat there, gritting my teeth, one eye on my watch, knowing I'd be late to pick you up! You think he cared?"

Poor Michael, I thought. It had to be awful having a father like his. I softened, as usual. I forgot all about my anger and said, "I'm sorry, Michael. It must have been awful."

He took my hand and held it against his cheek. "I don't know if I could take it, if it weren't for you. You're the only one I can talk to, the only one I can just be *me* with. You can't imagine what it's like when Dad's around. Even Mom's afraid of him."

"If you don't like the way he acts, how come you act just like him all the time!"

Michael bent his head. "I don't know. I don't want to be like him, but I can't seem to help it. Please forgive me."

"You're forgiven."

"I love you, Nicole. You know that."

"I know."

"If I ever lost you, I'd go crazy."

"You would not. Don't talk that way! People don't go crazy just because they break up. They're sad for a while, but they go on. We're both just high school kids. Don't get melodramatic!"

"Do *you* love *me*?"

I pulled at the loose button on my sweater. "Why don't we go home and we'll make popcorn and watch a video?"

He stared at me in the darkness without saying another word, then he started the car and we drove to my house.

It was always easier being alone with Michael at home because he relaxed. He often talked about his goals for the future while we did homework together, or fixed snacks, or just hung around. His dad expected him to become a professional tennis player for a few years, and after that go to college and become a successful lawyer or businessman.

"Is it what *you* want?" I asked once.

"Sure! I've *got* to be the best. I'll succeed at whatever I set my mind to. That's how my dad got to where he is. Do you know what it takes to make it in the record industry?"

I nodded.

"Dad's a fighter. *You* know what he says—"

" 'I was not delivered unto this world in defeat,' " I recited, echoing Michael. " 'Failure does not course in my veins.' " His father had made Michael and his brother repeat those words again and again, from the time they were seven. His mother tried to get his father to ease up on the boys, but he shushed her up, Michael told me.

That evening, after the party, I found it hard to get back into the old, comfortable mood we usually shared. Maybe it was because I was getting tired of having to deal with Michael's constant moodiness and problems. Maybe, too, because I had someone else to look forward to seeing now.

"I'm tired, Michael," I said around ten-thirty. "Would you mind going home?"

He hesitated, then said, "Sure. How about tomorrow?"

"We're going to see my cousins in the valley."

"How about later tomorrow, in the evening?"

I busied myself putting away the chess game we'd been playing. "I think we're staying for dinner."

"Will you phone if you get home early enough for me to come over?"

"Sure." I walked him to the door. " 'Night."

He put his arms around me and started to kiss me. I turned my face away.

"What's wrong?"

"Nothing. I just don't feel like that tonight." I tried to smile reassuringly.

He studied me a moment, then frowned. "Who is it, Nicole? Evan? Is it Evan? No? Shane?"

At Shane's name I felt all the blood rush from my face. "Stop fishing. I told you before, it's not your business. Good night, Michael. I'm going in."

"Wait! We have to talk about this! It's—*Shane*, isn't it?"

I hugged myself against the cold. Though I didn't admit or deny, my face must have given me away.

"I don't want you seeing anyone else, especially that Texas cowboy!"

"I'll see whomever I want!"

"No you won't!" Michael's tone turned sharp. "All right!" he said in a less threatening tone. "But you should know this by now! Failure isn't part of my vocabulary, Nicole!"

I stared into his determined but troubled face. " 'Night, Michael. I'm really exhausted. We'll talk tomorrow." I strode back into the house and shut the door.

CHAPTER
4

"**M**ICHAEL IS SUCH a nice young man," Mom said as we drove to visit Dad's cousins in Encino. She half turned to smile at me. "He taught Melanie to play chess. He always offers to help out, clearing dishes or setting the table. He's considerate and polite. I *trust* him. There aren't too many mothers who could say that about their daughters' friends."

I put my finger in the book I was reading, nodded, then went back to the book.

"Did you have a good time at the party last night?"

"So-so."

"Only so-so?"

"*Mom!*"

Sometimes Mom forgot. We had an agreement that now I was grown up and I didn't have to share everything that happened to me.

"Nicole doesn't like Michael anymore," my twelve-year-old sister, Melanie, announced, nudging me.

"What are you talking about?" I shut the book once more. "Sure I like Michael!"

"Do not!"

"Do too!"

"Then how come you told Evie you could hardly wait to see some new guy—*Shame*!"

"Shane!" I corrected, feeling my face redden. "I warned you, Melanie, if you ever eavesdropped I'd make mincemeat out of you!"

"Mom? Did you hear that?"

"Pipe down, you two. I can't drive when you're at each other," Dad said.

"Did too!" Melanie whispered. I gave her a warning nudge, then tried to go back to my book.

I really like Dad's cousins Louise and Norman. Even though they're pretty old, they're young inside. Norman is always excited about some new interest. If he doesn't have an answer to your question he rushes to his bookshelves and seems to have enough books to find the answer right away. Louise used to be a librarian, and I really feel I owe her a lot because she's the one who turned me on to books. They always brought me a book when they visited.

As soon as we got into the house and hugged all around and handed over the flowers we brought and hung up our jackets, Louise tapped my shoulder and told me, "Your friend Michael called a few minutes ago, Nicole. He wants you to phone him right back."

"Did he say why?"

"No, honey."

It can wait, I said to myself, annoyed.

"Who'd like a drink?" Norman asked, rubbing his hands together, when we went into the living room to sit down. The coffee table was loaded with Louise's specialties. Melanie instantly settled herself in front of the feast and began digging in. I sat on a chair, half listening to family talk and thinking with irritation about Michael. Why did he phone here? Was he checking on me when I was with my family?

When the phone rang a few minutes later Norman called, "It's for you, Nicole, your friend again!"

"Darn," I mumbled and went inside.

"Nicole? Hi!"

"What's up, Michael? Couldn't it wait until I got home?"

"Listen!" His voice crackled with excitement. "I just found someone who'll sell me tickets to that rock concert you've been dying to go to! I'm at his house right now. I need to know if you'll go!"

"Terrific! When?"

"Saturday!"

"Oh, *no*! This coming Saturday?"

"Right."

"I told you! I've got a date! You *know* that!"

"So cancel it! This is special! Make it another Saturday; it can't be that important."

"I can't!"

"Nicole. . . ." He sounded disappointed. "Don't be

26

like that! Do you know what it took for me to find these?"

We'd talked endlessly about finding tickets. The concert had been sold out for weeks. He must have turned the town upside down to get them. He knew if anything would make me break my date, this would be it.

"Buy the tickets, Michael. Don't miss this chance, but take someone else," I said. "Take Evie."

"You mean you *won't* go?" he asked, incredulous. "I don't believe it!"

"I can't. It wouldn't be right! Take Evie. She's crazy about the group too, and she's always fun to be with."

"I don't want to take Evie! I don't want to take anyone else! I want to take you! Darn you, Nicole!" he shouted, and then I heard the dial tone when he slammed down the receiver.

On Monday Michael seemed all over his sulk. He drove me and Evie to school, as if we'd never argued. I wasn't pleased that he'd hung up on me, but I let it go. Evie rolled her eyes at me to show her surprise and I just winked.

Evie peeled off to talk with Craig, her latest wounded bird. Michael and I walked on together.

"Okay, Nicole, you win," he said. "I won't escort you from class to class. Guess I have been a little too possessive." He smiled charmingly and I found myself so relieved I forgot all the harsh words of the weekend. "I've thought it over, and it's true. You have the right to date anyone you like. *And so do I.*"

For a second I felt grateful, but I also experienced an unexpected jolt of disappointment and alarm. Michael could easily find someone else. Did I really want to lose him?

For the rest of the week Michael seemed to be deliberately avoiding me. All the sudden freedom left me feeling a little lost. I knew he had the right, just as I did, but it hurt my ego. Could he give me up so easily?

"Last I saw of him he was talking with Beth," Evie told me when I asked if she'd seen him. "In the parking lot."

"*Beth?* Perfect Beth, the princess and beauty of the senior class?"

"Yep." Evie studied me for a reaction. "You're not jealous?"

"Of course not!"

"Good."

"Has he spoken to you about the concert tickets for Saturday, by any chance?"

"Nope. But I can't go anyway. I have a date Saturday, with Jeremy." She smiled in an embarrassed way.

"Is he the one—"

"No! That was Craig."

I suppressed a giggle, because I could tell by Evie's face that she was taking on yet another wounded bird. "What's Jeremy's problem?"

"He doesn't have one. Well, not exactly. It's just that he's been very upset since his parents split up. And I can help."

"Evie, Evie." I hugged my friend. "You're something else. You should be a psychologist."

"Where have I heard that before?"

We both laughed. And then we parted, and instead of thinking of Shane, as I'd been doing all last week, I found myself wondering what Michael was up to, and if he'd asked Beth to the concert I'd have loved to attend.

Saturday night I fussed with my curly hair for an hour, trying to get it to lie straight. It wouldn't. It sprang back into its own stubborn curliness minutes after I blow-dried it.

I tried on different skirts and jeans and tops and discarded everything. Why couldn't I be tall and willowy, instead of average and ordinary? I settled, finally, on a paisley skirt and coordinating sweater, grimaced at my face in the mirror, and decided I'd have to live with it.

A half hour, yet! I shook my wrists in anguish. Why was I so manic? I never got like this when Michael came over, not even from the very first date. A hundred doubts tumbled through my head. What if Shane and I couldn't find anything to talk about? What if he thought I was silly? What if, what if!

I hadn't even heard the bell ring when Melanie burst into my room without knocking. "He's here! Mom said to tell you. He's got a scar on his cheek, did you notice? I bet he was in a gang fight! Michael's much better looking!"

I stuck my tongue out at Melanie and swept by, carrying my jacket.

Mom sat on the couch in the living room quizzing

Shane. I hoped he wouldn't mind, because some people hated it when Mom got started. She can find out more about a person in five minutes than most people can in a year. Maybe it's being a reporter on our local paper that makes her that way. I call it "prying," but she says she's just curious about what makes people tick.

Shane stood up when I came in and gave me a warm smile. It eased the jumpy feeling in my stomach.

"Shane's been telling me about Texas and how tough it's been for the oil industry," Mom said. "Maybe I'll do a feature on his family for the paper."

"Careful around my mother, Shane," I said. "She's like a blotter. She sops up everything, and eventually it finds its way into print."

"Thanks for the warning. Now that I know, I'll embellish a little. Maybe a *lot*."

"See, Mom?" I said. "Told you you can't believe everything people say!"

Mom chuckled and fluffed a pillow. "Go on, you two. Have a good time, but don't be too late."

Shane took my hand as soon as we left the house. It felt comfortable, like we were old friends. He led me to an ancient, sort-of-silver VW at the curb. "My trusty steed, ma'am, Hi-Ho Silver!"

"Ah-hah!" I giggled. "It's only your *mother* who likes movies, huh?"

He threw me an appreciative grin, climbed in, and scrinched around in the bucket seat to look at me. "Let's talk about where we're going. But first, let me explain something."

I folded my arms, cocked my head, and waited.

"I just started working part-time at the Sport Chalet and haven't collected my first paycheck yet. Car insurance just came due and it's a big chunk, even for a car the age of Hi-Ho Silver. What I am trying to say is—I'd like to take you out to some really nice place, like you're probably used to . . . but all I can afford tonight is either a movie or eating someplace that's not fancy. Which would you prefer?"

I stared at him, amused by his honesty. Most kids I knew got allowances, or worked part-time. Michael always seemed to have lots of money to spend. His dad didn't believe in his sons wasting time working at low-paying jobs after school, when they could be improving themselves.

"I shouldn't have asked you out until I could really afford it—right?" Shane said. He watched me, anxiously.

I crooked my finger at him and started to get out of the car. "Come. . . ."

"Come? Where are we going?" He scrambled after me.

"Why spend money on a movie when we can go for a walk in the park two blocks from here? I'll show you around. It's really pretty. We've got feet. When we're tired and starving, we can go someplace for a snack. Are you game?" I started walking.

"Imp!" Shane called, and he was grinning. We started down the street, talking a mile a minute.

CHAPTER
5

I FOUND MICHAEL sitting on the front step when we got back from church Sunday. He leaped up as soon as we drove in and hurried over to our car.

"Michael!" Mom exclaimed, pleased. "How nice. Come in and join us for lunch!"

"Thanks, Mrs. Webber. Glad to."

Michael must have come from tennis practice, because he wore a white polo shirt and shorts. He looked tired, so the concert must have gone on till late, and I know he can't sleep in Sunday mornings. Mr. Donaldson insists the boys be on the courts with him by seven, no matter how late they've been up the night before.

We trekked into the house, and Mom went into the kitchen to start lunch. "Go entertain Michael. Dad will give me a hand," she said when I offered to help. "Go on, honey."

I took Michael out to the back and uncovered two patio chairs near the pool. "I'll get some juice, if you'd like," I offered.

"Sit down, Nicole. I don't want juice. Look what I brought you. Here." He handed me the concert program booklet from the night before.

"Ooooh," I exclaimed, delighted. "Oh, my goodness! *Thanks!*" The program was full of wonderful pictures and tidbits about the performers. I paged through it immediately. "Oh, Michael! You were sweet to bring it. Thanks! Thanks!" I squeezed his hand appreciatively. "May I keep it?"

"Sure! I brought it especially *for* you."

"Tell me! Was the concert terrific?"

"Super. Absolutely super! Went on until almost two!"

"Wow." I glanced at the program and asked casually, "Who'd you take?"

He shook his head. "You don't tell me who you went with; you don't find out who I went with."

"You went with Beth, right?"

He gave me an enigmatic smile. "How was *your* date?"

"Great. Really great."

"Shane kiss you?"

"None of your business!"

"Was it good?"

"Michael!"

"He did! I *know* he did!"

I laughed. "Oh sure you know. What a vivid imagination. How *could* you know? You were at the concert!"

"Right. I was at the concert." He touched my hand. "Okay. Let's stop this; I'm tired of it. You had your date. I had mine. We've had our little flings." He dug into his pocket and pulled out a small box. It was wrapped in gold foil with a tiny, pretty bow. "Here. Maybe this will show you how I feel."

"What?" My face got hot. He *wouldn't* buy me a *ring*! He wouldn't! I put my hands out to resist his offer. "I don't want any presents, Michael. Thanks, anyway."

"Take it!"

His tone intimidated me. Slowly, I unwrapped the foil and opened the box. Inside was a small, beautiful ring wrought with two love birds. Tiny red stones formed the eyes. It looked terribly expensive. "It's beautiful," I said, softly. "Really beautiful, but I can't take it."

"Of course you can!" He pulled the box away and removed the ring, then tried to fix it on my finger.

"No!"

"Why not?"

"Because I don't want it!"

"It's a *friendship* ring! That's all."

"I don't want it! I'm not ready for a ring, any kind of ring, Michael, please! I can't!"

His eyebrows knitted together in that tight, angry line I sometimes saw and always hated. "I bet you'd take it if Shane gave it to you, right?"

"No I wouldn't! I don't want a ring, any ring, from *anyone*!" I pushed the box away. "Let's go inside. Must be lunchtime."

"You always change the subject when I try to find out how you feel!"

"All right! You want to know how I feel, I'll tell you!" I looked away, trying to decide what to do. Dad always said, "Tell the truth. It may hurt at first, but in the long run it's best." But Mom doesn't agree. "The straight truth is too cruel," she says. "A spoon or two of sweetness with a hard-to-swallow truth takes the bite out of the unkindness."

"All right." Turning and looking straight up into Michael's dark, pained eyes I said, "I admire you and think you're absolutely terrific. You're thoughtful and always there for me. You're a very wonderful person—sexy, too." But not to me, I didn't add.

"I'm waiting for the ax to fall!"

"I love you, *in a way*, Michael. But . . ." I almost stopped because of the look on his face. "But not the way you want." I bit my lip.

Michael slammed his fist on the table so hard that it shook. "I knew it! I just wouldn't believe it! How could I have been so dumb? It's like my father always says! I can have all the facts right there in front of me and I refuse to see what they add up to!"

"Stop blaming yourself. It's not your fault. You've been wonderful to me."

"Not wonderful enough, obviously!" His voice broke.

I left my seat again and went to stand behind Michael. I put my arms around him, trying to be comforting, and said, "Please don't be sad. I'm sorry. I don't want to hurt you. Please, don't be sad."

Michael buried his face in his hands. I could feel his chest heaving like he might be crying. Scared, I pulled away. He hated for anyone to see him out of control. I walked off to the rose bushes, keeping my back to him.

In a few moments, Michael came to my side. "Our gardener trims the roses every January," he said, as if nothing bad had just happened. "It's amazing how fast the new growth comes. Mom brings flowers indoors by May, around prom time."

Prom time! Evie wondered if he'd ask. The word lay there between us like a bomb. *Please* don't ask me now, I pleaded silently. *Don't*, please.

"I guess I'm just going to have to try harder," Michael said, smiling at me. "There is *nothing* I can't do if I try hard enough. I love you, and I'm just going to have to figure out how to make you love me!"

"Oh, Michael. . . ." I let out my breath, half relieved, half annoyed. For a moment I thought that Dad's way was best—that I must tell him there was no chance, none at all. But I couldn't. Hope made him happy. How could I prick his happy balloon?

So I took the easy way, and said nothing.

Saturday morning I went to the Sport Chalet for a new pair of running shoes. The fact that Shane worked there, that he was assigned to the shoe section, of course had nothing to do with it.

The Chalet has the most amazing variety of outdoor equipment—climbing gear, camping, fishing, and ski stuff. This Saturday a huge crowd was gathered outside watching a mountain climbing demonstration. Three men, using pitons and picks were making their way up a fake mountain. It looked hard.

I watched for a while then let my eyes drift, looking in the crowd for someone I might know.

As soon as I went through the front door, I lost all interest in anything except finding Shane.

I wandered around, aimlessly examining this jogging outfit or that toboggan, but aware every instant of the salespeople nearby. Truth was, my chest got tighter and tighter the closer I got to sport shoes.

"May I help you?" someone behind me asked.

I swung around guiltily, and said, yes, I wanted to buy a pair of sneakers. For what? Tennis? Jogging? Walking? Or one of half a dozen other activities? "All of the above," I said.

And then Shane came out of the back with an armload of shoe boxes and my heart did something funny. I watched as he walked directly to his customer seated on a platform chair and began taking the shoes out for the man.

"Do you know your size?" the salesman asked.

I waved him off. "Let me look around a bit more. Thanks."

I edged toward Shane, hoping he'd see me, but he seemed totally absorbed. At last he wrote a sales slip, handed the box to the man, then bent to repack the other boxes he'd brought out.

"Hi, Shane," I said shyly, coming up to him.

He glanced up. "Nicole."

I smiled.

"What are you doing here?"

"Looking for a new pair of sneakers." I gestured to the dirty, worn ones I wore.

"Just let me put these away and I'll help you." He grinned back at me. "Wait now! Don't let anyone else near you! Be right back! You a seven?"

I nodded and took a seat while Shane disappeared into the stockroom. I removed my old sneakers and then sat back to wait.

From my seat on the platform I had a good view of the store. Young couples crowded the aisles, looking over the sporting goods. People stood in line at the cash registers. Some aisles away, near the Coleman camping equipment, a woman carrying a baby in one of those canvas pouches caught my eye. I smiled. And then my smile faded, because near her, watching me with an expression of absolute attention and irritation, stood Michael.

I felt as if all the blood drained out of my face.

"Well, here we go." Shane set four boxes on the floor beside my chair. "One of these should work. I'll have to take you hiking to break them in."

"Shane?"

He must have heard the strangeness in my voice because he looked up instantly.

"*Michael's* here."

"Really? Where?"

I pointed, but when I looked where I'd seen Michael

last, he wasn't there anymore. It gave me the eeriest feeling. I swallowed a lump of fear. "I think he's following me."

"Come on, Nicole. That's silly. He's probably here to buy something, just like you."

"I don't think so." I tried to shake my anxiety. Here I was with Shane, I shouldn't be talking about Michael. But the look on Michael's face!

Shane glanced around. "Why would he follow you?"

"I don't know."

"Relax. If he's here, it's no big deal. He wouldn't *follow* you! That would be weird."

"It *is* weird. Spooky!"

"Forget it. Here. Try this on. It should be perfect."

Shane helped me find the shoes I needed, but the thrill of being near him, of having him fit me personally, had lost something. An odd sense of uneasiness settled in place. Was Michael nearby even now— watching? He wouldn't really do that! Would he?

CHAPTER
6

I'D PROMISED, WHEN I couldn't go to the concert with Michael, that we'd spend the following Saturday together. Saturday came and I felt a revulsion at having to go through an evening with someone I didn't really want to be with anymore, even out of kindness.

I dragged myself into clothes with the enthusiasm of a slug, wishing I could tell a white lie and call it off. The bell rang, and I went to the door to let Michael in.

He stood there in a new blue windbreaker, as tall and good-looking as I'd ever seen him. His face held the same open eagerness it always had when he picked me up. I was surprised that some of my old pleasure of being with him returned.

We were going to a new movie—a Stephen King thriller. Michael loves them. He comes out of the theater all hyped up, laughing over the things that scare me most. I hate horror films. I sit with my face in my hands, or my head dug into Michael's shoulder when the awful gory stuff happens.

We stood in line to buy tickets. I'd sworn not to ask him, but I couldn't help myself. "What were you doing at the Sport Chalet this afternoon?"

He cocked his head playfully. "What were *you* doing there? Can't stay away from Texas?"

"I was buying sneakers! See?" I pointed to my feet.

"Sure. And I was buying—tennis balls!" He seemed annoyed, as if I wasn't being totally honest.

"In the camping section?" I lowered my voice because people nearby had stopped talking; maybe they were listening. "Michael, were you following me?"

"What if I was? Don't I have a right to know what I'm up against?"

"I don't want you checking on me, understand? What I do, when we're not together, is not your business! If we're going to remain friends—you're going to have to respect my privacy! Don't ever do that again!"

"Friends?" Michael returned. "We're more than *friends*!"

The line started moving toward the box office and there was no chance to answer. Then, when we got there, I stood aside, silently fuming, while Michael bought tickets. What did he mean—more than friends? We were not, anymore. I'd told him that.

Tickets in hand, Michael shepherded me inside and stopped to buy popcorn and drinks. We greeted kids we knew, then moved on into one of the theaters to find seats close to the front.

"This is going to be great! Even better than the last King. I predict you'll have your head on my shoulder for half the picture." He passed me a drink and held out the big container of popcorn, then glanced back to look for Joanie and Phil. They were joining us afterward to go to the Comedy House. "They're just behind us," he reported, satisfied.

"We are *not* more than friends anymore," I whispered, pushing away the popcorn. "I've already told you that."

"Ah, sweet Nicole. So sweet, so innocent." He leaned over and brushed my cheek with a kiss. "How can you even question it? Everyone knows—*everyone!*"

"Knows what?" I drew back and looked at him.

"That we were made for each other. Everyone knows that one day you and I will get married."

"Married!" My face burned and I glanced around, afraid people nearby had heard.

He put a finger on my lips and smiled. "Sssh. It's starting."

The lights dimmed; the curtain parted and the music began. Confused and frustrated, I turned to the screen as an ad for the *Los Angeles Times* appeared, and then a snack bar invitation, and then previews of coming films.

Oh, my God, I thought, unable to concentrate on any of it. I've got to stop this! I can't let him go on thinking like that! It's getting too crazy!

Right after the movie we joined Phil and Joanie and drove to the Comedy House. It's a kind of noisy club where you sit at small tables and get drinks and pretzels and watch comedy routines. In the car driving there Michael analyzed the film in great detail while I sat silently, subdued by the horror of what we'd just seen and troubled by how to deal with Michael's fantasy.

All through the comedy show Michael made remarks that cracked up Joanie and Phil more than the performers. They laughed so hard tears came to their eyes. "He's hilarious!" Joanie gasped. "Don't you think he's marvelous? Why aren't you laughing?"

Michael put an arm around my shoulders and pressed his cheek against mine. "Nicole's still getting over the movie. I shouldn't take her to films like that, but I love the way she gets when she's scared." For some reason that set Joanie and Phil laughing even harder. I forced a smile, then excused myself to go to the rest room.

"How about tomorrow afternoon?" Michael asked, as soon as we reached my front door. "We could go bike riding."

Shivering, I crossed my arms over my chest, and shook my head. "No." The evening had been horrible. I should have listened to my instincts and told him a white lie.

Michael placed his hands on my shoulders and smiled. "Okay, we could do something else. What would you like to do?"

"I don't want to go out with you anymore."

Michael's brown eyes turned black and the smile faded from his face. "Nicole, what are you saying? Did I do something wrong? I don't understand! Don't do this to me. Don't say awful things like that."

"You didn't say anything wrong, or do anything wrong. I just think we're seeing too much of each other."

He stared at me, letting my words sink in, then said, "Oh, okay. You need more space. I won't come over this week. All right? We won't get together tomorrow either. Next Saturday?"

"No. I don't want to go out with you anymore. Listen to me, Michael. It would be better if you stopped picking me and Evie up in the morning, too. I'm sorry. I don't know how else to say this, except straight out." I shivered. "I'm going in; it's cold."

Michael tried to wrap me in his arms, but I shook my head and pushed by to put the key in the door.

"Nicole, wait! I need you. I love you. Don't hurt me like this or I don't know what I'll do. You're the only person I love!"

"Stop it Michael! I don't want to hear that again. You're a terrrific guy but I don't love you. You just *think* you love me. Stop trying to convince me. You'll meet loads of girls before you really fall in love. Now please, let me by."

"Nicole!" he bellowed again. He tried to grab me.

"No! Leave me alone!" I clumsily unlocked the front door and rushed inside. I closed the door on him and stood against it, breathing hard.

"Nicole!" Michael pounded on the door.

"Go away, Michael! You'll wake everyone! Go away!" Tears started down my cheeks.

"Nicole!" Michael banged on the door, again and again. "Open up! Let me in! We have to talk! You can't do this to me. I won't let you."

"Go home, *please*! Be quiet and leave."

"You don't understand. You can't cut me off like this! I love you!"

"What's going on down there?" Dad rushed down the stairs, tying the belt around his robe. "Nicole? What is this?"

"It's Michael. He won't go home!" My chest felt like it would burst. "Daddy, do something! Please! I don't want to talk to him!"

"Go upstairs. Now!" Dad ordered.

I swept by and rushed up the stairs as he opened the door. Glancing back I saw Michael, trying to peer around Dad to see me, his face distorted by pain.

"Now, Michael," I heard Dad say kindly. "I don't know what this is about and I don't want to know. But it's after *one*! And I can't sleep with all this racket. Be a good fellow and go home. Whatever this is about you can straighten out tomorrow."

"Mr. Webber . . . please let me see Nicole. For just a minute."

"Go home, Michael. It's late and Nicole doesn't want to talk to you. Go on, son!"

I heard the front door close and then Dad's footsteps as he came back upstairs and went straight to his room. Michael knew which was my room, so I didn't turn on the light. My teeth began chattering and I couldn't stop them. I undressed in the dark and washed up, then went to the window and peeked out. Michael's car was still at the curb! He was leaning against it, gazing up at my window. I stuffed my fist in my mouth and bit hard. I don't know how long he stayed because I rushed back to my bed, covered my head with the blankets, and cried myself to sleep.

CHAPTER
7

"WHAT WAS ALL that about last night?" Mom asked at breakfast Sunday morning.

"I broke up with Michael and he wouldn't accept it." Tired from the night before, I nibbled at half an apple-spice muffin.

Mom put the newspaper down and looked at me in surprise. "You broke up with *Michael*? Why?"

I shrugged. "He's too—possessive."

"She likes Shane better now," Melanie said.

The phone rang. Its jangle went clear through me. That would be Michael, no doubt of it. Dad took his coffee cup and went to answer it.

"Hello, Michael," Dad said, watching me. "Thank you. I accept your apology." I shook my head vigorously. Dad sipped his coffee. "I'm sorry, Michael. Nicole can't come to the phone right now. Yes, try later; that would be best."

I let out my breath as Dad hung up and returned to the table. "See what I mean?" I cried. "He'll come over if I won't talk to him. Please, can we go somewhere today? Anywhere—just so we're not near the phone?"

"Wouldn't it be better if you did speak with him, honey?" Mom asked. "Hear him out? You've been friends a long time. Don't you owe him that?"

"No! If it made a difference I would, but Michael doesn't listen, Mom! He only hears what he wants to! And I have a right to my feelings."

Mom pursed her lips. "I think you're being very unkind."

I crushed the muffin crumbs into the plate. Just like her, always taking Michael's side, I thought. I stood up, taking my cup and plate with me. "Excuse me. I'll be in my room if anyone—*except* Michael—wants me. You might remember, Mom, I'm in the family, not Michael."

At first, I tried to write in my diary. I'm good about keeping it. Sometimes I write what I think of the books I read. Often I jot down something about who fictional characters remind me of in real life. I put down snippets of conversation from school that suggest story ideas, although I hardly ever get around to writing stories. Most of the time I write about my own life— what I do and think and feel.

Every time the phone rang, like every fifteen minutes, I'd look up and listen and get a nervous flutter. It would be Michael, just as I predicted. I'd told Dad to say that I didn't want to speak with him. There was nothing more to say.

Just before lunch Melanie knocked. "Phone call— for you, Dad says."

"Michael?" I dug myself deeper into the desk chair. "No."

"Okay, be right there." I closed my diary and went to the hall to answer.

"Is this Nicole Webber?" a woman's voice asked.

"Yes."

"I have a musical message for you." Without a pause she began to sing the Beatles song "Michelle," except that the name was changed to *Nicole*. "Nicole—my belle . . ." and so on. I rolled my eyes in embarrassment, but my heart sang. Shane and I had talked about that song just last week!

"Thank you," I said when she finished, feeling like I could hug the whole world. "Is there a message?"

"Yes. It says, 'I'm sorry. I was just kidding. Give me another chance. Love, Michael.' "

"Oh."

"We'll be happy to send you a copy of this," the woman said. "May I confirm your address?"

"No!" My voice came out sharper than intended. "No, don't bother." I hung up, felt Mom's questioning eyes on me, and just said, "Grrr!" as I went back to my room.

"Michael won't give up," I wrote in my diary. "And the harder he tries, the less I want to see him or have anything to do with him. What should I do? Should I talk to Evie about it? Shane?"

A few minutes later, the doorbell rang. Oh, please, not Michael, I thought, knowing I'd have to deal with him. I buried my head in my hands. Why hadn't I left the house, gone to Evie's, taken a walk—anything— not to be home. The bell rang again.

I went to the window, almost holding my breath, but instead of Michael's red Mustang out front, a green-and-white delivery van sat in the driveway. Sunday? A delivery truck?

Curious, I left my room and went down the hall to the landing overlooking the entry. Dad was accepting a big bouquet of red roses from someone I couldn't see. He started to close the door, when the delivery person said something. Dad waited, looking at the envelope attached to the bouquet. A moment later the delivery person returned with *another* bouquet—of white roses! I put my hand to my throat to still the sudden, hard beat. Dad closed the door and called, "Nicole!"

He looked up at me and winked. "Someone must like you a whole lot. Good gracious! Must be four dozen roses here! Come get them. They're making me—" He took a ragged breath, shuddered, and let out an explosive sneeze. Then he held the bouquets as far out of range as he could.

"My goodness! Oh, my!" Mom exclaimed when she came into the hall from the family room. She shook her head in wonder. "Michael?"

"No doubt." I took the flowers from Dad and went to the kitchen to look for vases. Mom and Dad followed.

"Open the envelope!" Mom urged. "Aren't you curious?"

I laid the bouquets on the counter and opened the envelope with the red roses. The little card inside read, "From the heart. Michael." I opened the envelope with the white roses. The card said, "You are fire and ice to me. You are the moon and the stars. You are everything. Shut me out and I'll die." Face burning, I hurriedly slipped the cards into my jeans pocket.

Mom brought two vases to the sink and began filling them with water. "The boy adores you, honey. Just look at this. These flowers must have cost a fortune. He's so sweet."

"It's not *his* money," I said, nastily. "It's not like he 'earned' it. He gets a huge allowance, no questions asked, so long as he wins tennis matches. In other words, his father *buys* him, just like Michael's trying to *buy* me! He's not sweet. He's awful."

"Nicole!"

"Marsha, stay out of it," Dad said. "Maybe the boy *is* manipulative. There's no use in Nicole stringing him along if she's no longer interested. Leave her alone."

"Right," I said, grateful to Dad. I agreed with him one hundred percent. I wished Mom wasn't blind to Michael's faults. I hadn't realized until this moment that Michael had always persuaded me to his viewpoint when we argued by bringing me some small gift and apologizing. It had been so flattering. No other girl I knew who was my age had a boyfriend so generous. When I told some of my friends about how he'd act their eyes would widen with envy and awe. Even Evie thought it was great.

"You know what I feel like doing with these?" I asked when Mom brought the water-filled vases to me. I didn't wait for an answer. "This is what I feel like doing!" I gathered both bouquets in my arms and marched out the kitchen door to the garbage pails.

"Nicole!" Mom cried, hurrying after me. "Nicole, don't!"

I lifted the lid of one of the cans and held the flowers over it. Maybe Michael was close by, watching, listening. "These don't change a thing, Michael," I said, loud enough to be heard at the next house. "I don't want any more of your gifts. It's over. Just leave me alone!"

"Nicole, no!" Mom grabbed the flowers from my hands, her tone full of outrage. "You can't do this! He's trying to apologize. You're terrible! How can you be so heartless?"

I stepped back, wiping my hands on my jeans. "You want the flowers? Great! They're yours! But put them in *your* room, Mom, because if I see them anywhere else, I'll puke!" I turned and marched back into the house, out of breath from anger and frustration. Phone calls, singing messages, flowers. He figured he'd break through to me one way or another. He always had. But not this time! He wasn't going to buy me. Not at any price.

CHAPTER
8

THE PHONE CALLS stopped.

The messages stopped.

Michael didn't try to reach me for the rest of the weekend. With each hour of silence, I breathed more freely.

Then Evie phoned late Sunday afternoon.

"Michael's been calling me *all* day," she reported. "He said you refuse to talk to him. He begged me to tell you he was just kidding about getting married and living happily ever after. He went on and on about how if you don't love him, it's okay. He'll live with it, but he doesn't want to lose you as a friend."

"Oh, sure," I said, though a seed of doubt began to take root.

"I told him, 'Michael. Don't put me in the middle.

I'm not going to be your go-between. Work it out with Nicole yourself.' Was that okay?''

"Did he sound very upset, Evie?" I got a lump in my throat just asking that question. "I mean—I know him so well. When he's really upset, he tells me these things that are just terrible, and then he laughs, as if it doesn't hurt at all!"

Evie didn't answer for a moment, then said, "Yeah. He laughed, especially when he told me what you shouted when you threw out the flowers."

"Ohhh . . ." I was almost feeling sorry for Michael, until I realized he had to have been watching me if he knew what I said when I dumped the roses. He'd been watching from somewhere nearby. He had it bad for me, but it wasn't my fault if I didn't love him. Why couldn't he just leave me alone?

Monday morning, as soon as the bell rang for lunch, I gathered up my books and dashed out of my algebra class. I half expected, despite everything that happened, to see Michael rushing from his last class so we could walk together to the cafeteria.

When I reached the lunchroom, some of the usual crowd was already seated at "our" table. I peered around the kids in line and saw Michael up front, loading his tray with food.

"Hi, Nicole," a voice in front of me said.

"Oh! Hi, Evan."

"Why don't you go ahead? No one will mind. Michael will let you in."

"No, no. That's all right."

We talked about this and that as the line moved forward, and all the time I grew more and more anxious, because this would be the first time in many months that I didn't plan to sit with Michael and the group.

Evan paid for his lunch then waited until I paid for mine. "Why don't you go on," I said, looking around for Evie. She had offered to find seats as far from Michael as possible, since she always got to the cafeteria first.

"Aren't you coming?"

"No."

Evan raised an eyebrow, understanding immediately, and went off to his usual table.

Lunch tray in hand, I wandered around until I spotted Evie. She was far in the back standing up, waving her arms wildly and pointing at someone beside her who also stood and waved. Shane!

I glanced only once and quickly in Michael's direction. When our eyes met he looked away. The seat beside him, the one I usually occupied, was vacant. I hurried to join Evie and Shane.

Without Michael in my life the days opened up. Instead of the predictable, each day offered surprises. I took real pleasure in time alone, quiet time, time to think and dream and read. I read more books Shane sometimes suggested, so that we'd talk about them afterward.

Shane came to the library when he wasn't working. I found myself looking for him, hoping he'd come. Afterward we'd go out for a frozen yogurt in Old Town

Pasadena. Most of the time we'd talk—not about kids we knew at school or our family situations, as I had with Michael. Shane would tell me about the story he was working on or about college plans.

"You know what I'd like to be?" I admitted one evening, watching his face to see if he'd laugh.

"What?"

"An astronomer." Michael had laughed and said there was no money in it, and why would I want to spend my life with eyes glued to a telescope? Then he'd added that if I really wanted to it was okay with him.

"An astronomer? No kidding!" Shane looked half surprised, and yet his expression showed admiration. "I can see why! The heavens are *full* of fantastic secrets. It would be a fascinating career."

I squeezed his hand, feeling as if I were walking two feet off the ground.

"Know what we should do?" he asked, and then continued, "Next Saturday, we'll go to The Griffith Observatory. There's a special exhibit in the planetarium on the *Voyager 2* flight to Neptune. You'll enjoy that."

"Oh yes! But would *you*?" I was so used to doing what Michael wanted, without even thinking what I'd prefer, that it seemed odd, selfish even, to accept.

"Of course I would!" Shane exclaimed. "I'll learn something new, and you'll be there with me. How could I not enjoy it?"

Shane picked me up early Saturday evening. The Griffith Observatory is on a hilltop in the Los Feliz district, past beautiful private homes and up a winding road. It was a clear night with a dry, fragrant breeze, unusual for February.

"What a perfect evening," I said, as we climbed the road from the parking lot to the terrace outside the observatory. The warm winds carried a desert scent to us. The mountains were silhouetted against the bright night sky; it was so clear you could read by the light of the moon.

We bought tickets for the nine o'clock show, and since we had some time we looked down on a sparkling city. Shane's arm encircled my shoulders and I leaned into him, feeling warm and happy.

"There's the Big Dipper." I pointed to the heavens. "And the Pleiades."

"Pleiades?"

"Those stars, over there. Even though you can only see six stars, actually, there are seven, named after the seven daughters of Atlas in Greek mythology."

He moved behind me, placed his cheek against mine and asked, "Where?"

I kissed his cheek, and was so truly happy I closed my eyes to register the moment.

"Well!" Shane said, suddenly. "I don't believe it, but isn't that *Michael*, with Beth, coming up the path?"

I stiffened. "Where?" I looked down the path. "Oh my goodness, yes!"

"Did you tell him we'd be here tonight?"

"Of course not!" I swung around, the intimacy, the magic gone. I'd wanted so much for this to be a special evening, just the two of us. "Hurry! Let's go inside before he sees us!" I tugged at Shane's arm.

"Nicole! Shane! Wait up!" Michael called, just as we went through the door into the observatory lobby.

"Oh-oh," Shane said. "They've spotted us. May as well be pleasant."

Michael and Beth came panting to our side. "Poof! We really ran!" Michael fanned himself with a hand. "Didn't you hear me?"

"Isn't this amazing? I thought Michael was so original suggesting we come here," Beth said. "And here we meet you two!"

I glared at Michael. "It *is* amazing! Very!"

"I read that the show ends next week," he explained, talking to Shane, not me. "I remembered how much Nicole's dad talked about the work he did on *Voyager*, so I thought, This is something you just don't miss!"

Oh, sure, I thought, not believing him for one second.

"We're going inside," Shane said. "Better get tickets."

"Right! Save us seats, will you, Shane?" Michael grabbed Beth's hand and rushed off to the ticket booth.

I rolled my eyes in a gesture of hopelessness.

"Give him a break, Nicole. He's with Beth. What he said about why he's here makes sense. Michael's okay. Don't be so hard on him."

It had been two weeks since I'd spoken with Michael. He seemed to have made a terrific adjustment to our breakup. Beth really seemed to like him, and

I'd heard they spent time together. I didn't know what to think. Maybe his being here was perfectly innocent. Maybe I enjoyed thinking he couldn't get over me! Still, I resented his cutting in on my evening with Shane.

Once the show began I forgot all about him. The itty-bitty spacecraft, weighing less than most cars, traveled through space for *twelve* years! Over four *billion* miles into space and it winds up less than twenty miles from where it was supposed to be! I was awed. It whizzes by Neptune, going thirty-eight thousand miles an hour, snaps pictures like a shutter-happy tourist, and a few hours later we get to see what no one ever saw before!

When the lights came back on I was still four billion miles away with a zillion questions. I couldn't wait to talk to Dad.

Shane took my arm as we left the theater. Michael scurried to my other side. "What did you think, Nicole? Wasn't it fantastic?" We started down the hill to the parking lot. "Nicole's father *managed* the Voyager project!"

"Really?" Beth managed, trying to be included in the conversation.

I clamped my mouth shut, thinking, What's he trying to do? Show off how much he knows about my life?

"Well, here we are," I said. We'd reached the parking lot and I hoped now we could say good-bye.

"You guys want to go out for a bite? I know a great Thai place near here, *not expensive,* either," Michael added, maybe for Shane's sake. "How about it?"

I did *not* want to spend the rest of the evening with Michael and Beth.

"Thai food! I love it," Shane said, but then he checked me. "I don't know. We had other plans. It's up to Nicole."

"Oh, come on! It's too early to go home and we're all hungry and this place is *fantastic*! We'd love you to join us, wouldn't we, Beth?"

Beth's smile looked forced.

"Say yes, Nicole; be a good sport, *please*? It'll be fun!" Michael put an arm around Beth.

"What do you say, Nicole?" Shane asked.

Shane wanted to go; I could hear it in his voice. Michael really seemed to like Beth. Should I give him the benefit of the doubt? Every instinct said no. But I wanted to please Shane, and not embarrass Michael. "Oh, all right!" I said finally, hating myself for being a wimp and not listening to my instincts.

The Thai restaurant was small. The room, with deep red carpeting, was inviting and there were intricately carved chairs and white cloths on the tables. It smelled of strange and exotic spices. We each ordered a different dish, so we could share and taste four things.

Beth and I went off to the rest room to wash up. We stood side by side at the mirror, she brushing out her beautiful auburn hair, I washing my hands. Before I could think of a thing to say to make conversation Beth started talking.

"I know what you're thinking," she said, dropping her brush back into her purse. "You think Michael knew *you'd* be at the observatory, and that's why we came. Well, think again, because that's not the reason!"

The venom in her tone brought goose bumps to my arms. "I sure hope so."

"My goodness! I always thought you had a big ego and now I'm sure. Michael's a wonderful guy! He told me what happened between you two."

I turned off the faucet and held up my wet hands, not daring to move an inch to get a towel. I stared at Beth in the mirror. "He did?"

"Yes, he did! He told me how you lost interest in each other; happens all the time. Just like it happened with Jimmy and me. So stop acting like he's chasing you! He's not! He's interested in me!"

"That's great." I could barely control the waver in my voice. Love must be blind for her not to see the truth, I decided. But then, maybe he did like Beth, a lot, and it was sour grapes on my part. I dried my hands, picked up my purse, and we left the rest room. I hoped she was right.

When we got to the table Michael was talking about tennis, cracking Shane up with funny stories about players he knew. Beth slipped into her seat, and I noticed she reached for Michael's hand under the table. Michael was being charming, Michael Funny-Guy, the Michael everyone at school recognized and liked.

The food arrived, and for the next half hour we mostly talked about how good it was. Shane wanted us to describe the tastes with words. Tastes are hard to explain, but we all had fun trying.

After dessert Michael turned to me for the first time

since we sat down. "Nicole? Do you remember the first time I took you to a fancy restaurant? And do you remember our first ice-skating date? You kept falling all over me." He laughed and went on telling about other dates, fun things we'd done together that would have been better left unsaid in front of Beth and Shane. His eyes danced; his voice got louder and more excited. I tried to signal him to stop, but he just went on as if he didn't notice. Shane began drawing designs in a spilled packet of sugar on the table and Beth stared down at her plate. Michael's behavior was so inappropriate we were all embarrassed and appalled.

"It's late," I said, finally, desperate. "Shane? Shouldn't we be going?"

"Yes. Yes, of course. I promised to get Nicole home early." Shane jumped to his feet, glanced at the bill, and took some money from his wallet. "This should cover our share."

Beth wound a napkin around and around one finger, avoiding our eyes.

"It's still early!" Michael protested.

"Not for me." I slid out of the booth. "Have fun, you two. See you at school." I wanted to run, not walk, to the nearest exit.

Shane took my arm when we reached the street. "Now I see what you mean! He couldn't stop talking about you! He's got it bad!"

"I know! I know!" I cried, exasperated. "So what should I do? Tell me, Shane! How can I turn him off?"

CHAPTER

9

I GOT HOME after midnight. Almost immediately, the phone rang. I ran to answer it before it woke Mom and Dad.

"Nicole?"

"Michael!" I whispered. "Why are you calling? Do you know what time it is?"

"Wait! Don't hang up! I've got to talk to you!"

"Tomorrow! I'm going to bed. You were positively horrible tonight. I don't *want* to talk to you! Good night!" I hung up. Before I could walk more than a few steps, the phone rang again.

"What do you *want*?" I asked, exasperated.

I didn't get an answer, only a muffled sound, like crying. "Michael? Mi-chael! What's wrong?" I waited, anxious and worried. Had he just had a fight with his father? Once, he'd been so down after one of those that he'd talked about suicide. Scared, I'd listened and advised and chided and tried to comfort him until he calmed down.

"Michael . . ." I begged, gently. "Tell me. Are you okay? What happened? Talk to me!"

"I can't stand it," he murmured, so low I hardly heard. "I feel like chucking it all."

I got a tight feeling in the pit of my stomach. "Come on! Nothing can be that bad!"

"You don't understand; you can't possibly!"

"Try me. Come on."

"You hate me! I could see it in your eyes! Everything I do lately goes wrong! It's not worth it! I want *out*!"

I shuddered. "Michael—please, listen. I don't hate you. Honestly. Please don't talk like that, it scares me!" The words tumbled out while I tried to think what to do. When he'd talked like this before, he knew I'd be there for him. Now, he had no one to unload on. Was he really threatening suicide? Would he really take his own life? Did he mean it? Should I keep him talking and get to another phone to call the police?

"Seeing you and—and Shane together, it suddenly became clear. I knew who to blame! It's all *his* fault! *He's* the one who turned you against me! I hate him! I *hate* him! I could *kill* him!"

"You don't mean that!" I felt faint. "Michael! That's crazy! You *wouldn't* hurt Shane! It wasn't his fault! Not anyone's. Where are you, Michael? Where are you calling from?"

"*Why?*"

He knew why I'd asked. "We have to talk!"

"We *are* talking. What more is there to say? You avoid me. You flaunt Shane! You don't care a fig about me now! What's to say?"

"I care. Do you think I'd be talking to you at this hour of the night if I didn't? Now stop talking nonsense about ending things. You've plenty to live for."

"I don't! I don't care about *anything* anymore!"

"Darn you! Quit feeling so sorry for yourself!" I bit my tongue, immediately regretting my outburst. "Michael?"

Silence.

"Michael? Talk to me!"

"Good-bye, Nicole."

"Wait! Wait!" My voice rose to a shriek. Too late. I heard the dial tone.

I stared out the family room door to the moonlit patio and the pool beyond, still clutching the phone, biting my lip. I'd said all the wrong things. I should have told him to come over and talk. Face-to-face I could have calmed him. All kinds of horrible possibilities rushed through my head. Michael knew how to use his father's gun! What if he went into the garage and . . . What if he got into the car and floored the gas pedal? If anything happened, it would be my fault!

Call him; get him back on the phone, my head ordered. But what if he wasn't there? What if he wouldn't listen? What if his mom or dad answered?

Should I? Shouldn't I? Paralyzed with uncertainty, I still held the phone, and then realized I had no choice. With trembling fingers I dialed Michael's home. If he was there, surely he'd pick up the phone right away so he wouldn't wake his parents. If he wasn't, what then?

The phone rang two, three, four times. Please answer; please answer! I begged silently, imagining Michael standing right there, deliberately not picking it up just to scare me.

"Hello?" At last! Michael's father!

"Mr. Donaldson, this is Nicole. I know it's very late, but may I speak with Michael please? It's terribly important."

"It's after midnight, young lady! He's out on a date!"

"He phoned me just a minute ago; I don't know from where. He was very upset. I need to speak with him. Maybe he's home. Would you please go look?"

Mr. Donaldson set the phone down and for the next few minutes I stared at the bulletin board on the wall. The loudest sound in the room was my heartbeat pounding in my ears.

Mr. Donaldson came back on the line. "He's not in his room, Nicole, so he must have called from someplace else."

"Would you see if his car is in the garage, please? I know this sounds strange, but would you please?"

"What is this about, Nicole?" Mr. Donaldson demanded. "He's not home. I told you."

I pictured Michael in his car, in the garage, only feet away from the telephone, maybe dying—and his father wasting time, unwilling to check. I suppose he could have been any number of other places, but the garage worried me most of all. "Michael sounded desperate when he phoned. He talked about killing himself!"

"Bosh!" Michael's father pronounced. "Michael kill himself? Ridiculous! My son's the most disciplined, self-confident young man you will ever meet. He'd never do something like that!"

"Mr. Donaldson, believe me! We had an argument. I broke up with him."

"Come now, Nicole! Aren't you being a bit dramatic? My son would never hurt himself, especially not over—a *girl*!"

"Oh, please, look in the garage! *Please!*"

Mr. Donaldson hesitated. To look he'd have to go downstairs and then outside. "If Michael phoned from here, he would be in his room, *not* in the garage! It's almost one o'clock in the morning, young lady! I'm going back to bed and I advise you to, also! Good night!"

He hung up, just as Michael had done, leaving me biting my thumbnail, not knowing what to do next. Surely Mr. Donaldson wouldn't go to bed before checking the garage, even though he considered it ridiculous? Surely?

I struggled with myself. Did I believe that Michael might actually kill himself? Yes, I did. Sure he was charming and funny, but deep down he was terribly insecure. Should I call the police? Should I wake Dad and ask him what to do? Should I phone Shane and ask him to go looking for Michael's red Mustang? Every minute I wasted worrying might make a difference.

Finally, I could stand it no longer. I slipped into

Mom and Dad's bedroom and touched Dad gently on the shoulder. When he didn't react, I did it again.

"Huh? What?" He sat up abruptly, recognized me, and whispered, "Nicole!" He glanced toward Mom, sleeping soundly at his side.

I put a finger to my lips and beckoned him to follow me.

Without a word he eased out of bed, pulling on his robe, and left the room, closing the door quietly behind him.

He walked down the hall to my room.

Whispering, though Mom couldn't possibly hear, I told Dad about Michael's phone threat, and about my call to his father. "I'm afraid, Daddy! Michael might be in that garage right now doing something terrible to himself! Do you think I'm crazy?"

"No," Dad said. "You don't ignore a suicide threat."

"Can we go over there *now* and check?"

Dad shook his head. "We can't just drive onto someone's private property and open his garage in the middle of the night. Donaldson might think we were thieves and come after us with a shotgun."

"Then what *can* we do?" I pressed my hands to my face, shivering.

"What's the Donaldsons' number?" Dad asked. "Come on. I'll talk with his father."

Together we hurried down the stairs to the family room phone. I dialed Michael's home and handed the receiver to Dad, then stood there watching his face.

"Yes, hello Mr. Donaldson," Dad said, rubbing his eyes with one hand. "This is Jerry Webber, Nicole's father. Now wait! Hear me out!" Dad's voice rose. "I know it's very late and I'm sorry to wake you again, but we're talking about your son's life! I don't think it's too much to ask to go out to the garage and see if he's there!

"I understand he went out on a date with another girl. I understand!" Dad exclaimed, impatient now. "But he phoned my daughter a little while ago and Nicole believes . . . Mr Donaldson!" Dad hissed. "Would you rather I called the police?"

That must have done it because Dad nodded, put his hand over the receiver, and winked at me. "He's going to look. I'm sure it'll be all right." I stuffed my fist against my mouth and pressed. Dad put a hand on my shoulder and we waited.

"He isn't? Well, good!" Dad said at last. I let out the breath I'd been holding and glanced up hopefully. "I certainly hope he'll be home soon, but I'll tell you. If it were my son, I wouldn't take any chances. I'd be out in my car right now—combing the neighborhood for him!"

Dad hung up and put an arm around me as we walked back up the stairs. "Do you think he'll go look for Michael?" I asked.

"I wouldn't be surprised. But there's nothing more we can do. So you just go to bed now and stop worrying, honey. Michael's probably driving home right now."

We'd reached my bedroom. "Thanks Daddy." I hugged Dad hard, feeling the rough texture of his terrycloth robe against my cheek, still not really satisfied. "I'm sorry I woke you."

"It's okay, sweetheart. You did the right thing. Now let's get some sleep."

At the door to my room I said, "Please don't tell Mom."

His eyes looked sad and I could tell he wanted to object, but he nodded.

I went into my room. The moonlight made a circle of light on the beige carpeting and a breeze ballooned the curtains inward. I went to the window, parted the curtains, and stared out to the street. Could Michael possibly be nearby, watching? Before, I would have thought that bizarre, but now I *wished* it. From my bedroom window I studied every shadow, jumped when a breeze stirred a nearby bush, held my breath when a car drove slowly down the block and parked.

Finally, believing he wasn't near, I undressed and lay in bed. I stared at the ceiling, a heavy lump of tears in my throat. Whenever I heard a siren, my heart leapt. When the next-door neighbor's dog barked, I ran to the window to look out again. In the long hours of worry, I made a pact with myself. If Michael was okay, I would try to be his friend. I couldn't take the chance that he would kill himself. He'd get over me. He had everything to live for and so did I.

CHAPTER
10

I AWOKE SUNDAY morning to a mockingbird singing in the pine outside my window and the muffled sound of voices from downstairs. For a moment I just listened, wondering how many different trills the mockingbird could imitate, then all the things that went on the night before rushed back into my head.

I groaned, pressing my face into the pillow, wondering if Michael was all right, remembering the vow I'd made just before falling asleep. I wanted to curl up into a ball and shut everything out, but instead forced myself to a sitting position and reached over to turn on the clock radio. If anything happened, the local news station would broadcast it. I tuned the radio low and sat on the edge of my bed, hugging myself against the fear.

"Area residents are invited to a concert on the green

between four and six P.M. today at Ocean View Park, corner of Foothill and Ocean View," the announcer said. "The public is invited to a seven P.M. meeting Tuesday at Descanso Gardens, where final arguments on the Sport Chalet's expansion plans will be heard. And now for the local news." I straightened up.

"Vandals broke into the home of Mr. and Mrs. Orson Brown at four-fifteen Commonwealth last night. Damage is estimated at two thousand dollars. A fire broke out at . . ."

Eyes on the radio, I listened with every cell in my body until the public announcements began. *Nothing about Michael!* I dropped back onto my bed like a rag doll, exhausted.

I couldn't stand not knowing another second, and yet didn't want to phone Michael and get his father again. Could Shane help?

"Just the person I wanted to talk to," he said as soon as he heard my voice. "How would you like to go to Universal Studios today? I got free tickets!"

For an instant the heaviness lifted. "Oh, boy, would I!" I almost cried. But then I thought, how could I go out and have a good time until I knew Michael was safe?

"I don't hear you jumping for joy, Nicole. Is there a problem?"

"Yes, but I can't say what right now." It didn't seem proper to tell anyone, even Shane, about Michael's suicide threat. What if it got out? There'd be people who would always think less of Michael, and others who would be angry at me for causing his pain. "Could you do me a favor without asking questions?"

"I guess. . . . What?"

"Michael called me when I got home last night and he sounded upset. Would you phone him and let me know if you talk to him?"

"I thought you didn't want to see or talk to him ever again?"

"I don't, but I can't help feeling a little worried about him. Look, you said you wouldn't ask any questions."

"All right. But what do you want me to say? I can't just call him without a reason."

"Talk about tennis. I don't care. Don't mention last night. Just let me know if he's home."

"Okay. . . ." Shane sounded doubtful. "I won't ask what this is about. I'll do it, but I think it's pretty strange! Call you right back."

I sat on the edge of my bed, one hand on the receiver, ready to pluck it up at the first ring. Melanie knocked at my door.

"Nicole!" she called out, "Mom's making Belgian waffles. She wants to know if you're coming down soon!"

"Five minutes!" I answered.

"Can I come in?"

"No!" The phone rang and I grabbed for it, hoping Melanie wasn't standing at the door, trying to listen.

"Shane? Did you talk to him?"

"Yes."

"Oh! Thank goodness!" I put a hand to my throat

and closed my eyes, smiling. "Did he say anything about last night?"

"Yeah. Apparently, his mother woke him. For a while it didn't even sound like him; his voice was thick, like he might be pretty hung over."

"Ummm," I said, encouraging him to go on.

"He apologized for being such a bore at dinner, monopolizing the conversation. Said he was probably in big trouble with you, that you'd never want to talk to him again. Said his father really chewed him out when he got home."

"Then he's okay!"

"Sure, why? Did you think he wouldn't be?"

"Did he say anything else?" I asked, instead of answering his question.

"Nicole, I don't like this. If you wanted to talk to Michael, why didn't *you* call? I'm not a messenger boy! *What did he say? Did he say anything else?* It sounds like you're still stuck on the guy. Are you?"

"No!"

"Then why are you checking on him like this? Why didn't *you* call him?"

"Because . . . Because he called me late last night and threatened to kill himself!" I covered my mouth with my hand and stared at the wall in horror.

"Oh!" Shane replied. "Oh, wow!"

For the longest time neither of us spoke. Then Shane said, "I don't know what to say. I didn't realize . . ."

"Don't say anything and forget what I told you. Let's change the subject, please. I'm sick of it!"

"All right. Do you want to go with me to Universal Studios? I could pick you up in an hour."

"I'd love to, Shane! Yes. See you soon."

A few minutes later, at breakfast, Mom asked the usual questions: Did you have a good time? Where did you go? What time did you get home? I gave her the headlines, but none of the details. When she heard Michael and Beth showed up and went to dinner with us she said, "Oh, how nice!"

Dad passed my chair and touched my shoulder. I looked up to read the question in his eyes. "He's okay!" I whispered. He squeezed my shoulder, smiled, and went to get more coffee.

I dressed in jeans and a red T-shirt Melanie had given me for Christmas, which read, MISSION POSSIBLE: ASTRONAUT-E. Mom or Dad must have helped her make that up. When Shane arrived, I grabbed my windbreaker and ran downstairs, calling out to Mom when I might be home.

Shane opened the car door for me. "Have you heard from Michael?" he asked.

"First rule. We are not to use the M word again today!"

"No problem." Shane smiled, then his forehead wrinkled into a worried frown. "Without Mmmmmm, what else can we talk about?"

I punched him playfully on the arm and giggled. "Here's something," I said, as we drove off. "How did you get that scar on your face? Melanie says you must have been in a gang fight, but I think you probably were in the foreign legion."

I could see his lips curve into a grin and he took one hand off the steering wheel to touch the light line that ran down the right side of his face. "Actually, Melanie's closer. I was captured by aliens and tortured for the military secrets they thought I had."

"Oh, sure! Try again!"

"How can you doubt me? You haven't seen *all* my scars. I'm really a robot, you see, in a human shell."

I laughed, and scrunched around in my seat to look at him. "I can see you have a fine imagination, young man. You're destined to become a writer!" I said, trying to imitate a teacher we knew. "Come on, Shane; what really happened?"

We were driving down the 2 freeway into Glendale. A fine drizzle misted the windshield. I hoped it would let up before we got to Universal.

"I fell off my tricycle when I was three—and have hated heights ever since." Shane glanced quickly my way. "Not very original or exciting."

Soon we drove into the parking lot at Universal and wound our way up the levels till we found a parking space. For an instant I thought of Michael. He never wanted to take me on the Universal tour because he'd done it so often. Whenever guests came to town he "had" to take them on his father's orders. I'd been there with my family when I was a little kid. I wondered if it had changed much.

Universal Studios is on a hilltop in Universal City.

It's the place where television shows and movies are made. Tourists get bused around to see how it's done. Half of the tour is by tram and on foot; for the other half you're free to take in any of the "shows," such as stuntmen and animal performers.

We were lucky, and got on a tour right away. The tram took us through movie sets of old Western towns and European villages and New York streets that were only fronts. We nearly got gobbled up by the shark from *Jaws,* washed out by a raging river, and buried alive in a tunnel where a very realistic earthquake shook the tram and broke power lines and support beams. I became completely involved and didn't think of Michael at all.

When we reached the *Star Trek* building an official-looking person in a commander's uniform asked if we'd like to be in the show. Shane looked at me and I at him and together we nodded our heads. "Yes!"

They took us backstage and dressed us and gave masks to some of the others and made us up like characters in the show. I got to be an engineer on the *Star Trek* spaceship, and Shane wound up as an alien wearing a greenish mask and flipperlike feet. We rehearsed our few lines, then went onstage before maybe a thousand people and performed with live cameras taping us! At the end of the show we sat back down in the audience and saw our scenes put together with actual clips from *Star Trek,* so it looked like we were really part of the show!

"Oh, wow! Wasn't that fun? I never laughed so much in my whole life!" I exclaimed as we followed the crowd out of the theater. "You looked so funny! You were such a ham!"

"Me, a ham? What about you? You giggled all the time you said your lines!"

"Did not!" Grinning, I glanced around to see if people behind us heard what he said. A man with a small child on his shoulders smiled at me. "Did you see him?" I pointed at Shane. "He was in the show—that green, slimy alien!"

The crowd moved forward and I couldn't really talk without getting trampled on, so I turned back to Shane, holding on to his jacket and trudging along. Suddenly, a rush of fear almost took my breath away practically knocking me cold. Michael was here! I saw him! In the brief moment I'd turned I had glimpsed him far off to the left. He was dressed in his old army fatigue jacket and cap.

I swung around suddenly, and looked again. My eyes swept the crowd: mothers and fathers and grandparents with children, couples like us, Japanese visitors, all pouring out of their seats into the aisles—but no one in a camouflage jacket that I could see. I remembered that day at the Sport Chalet. Now you see him, now you don't!

I tugged at Shane, pushing along in front of me. He glanced back. "I think Michael's here!"

He gave me an impatient look. "I thought you weren't going to mention him again!"

"I think he's following us."

"Oh, come on, Nicole!"

Outside the *Star Trek* building Shane stepped aside,

letting the crowd by. He took my hand. "All right, we'll wait. If it is him, we'll ask him what's going on!"

I strained to scan each face moving by, my heart beating so hard I felt my throat pulsating. For ten minutes we waited while the audience emptied out of the building. I wanted to see Michael just to prove I wasn't paranoid. But Michael never came out, nor did we see anyone dressed as I'd described.

"Satisfied?" Shane turned to me. "He's really got you spooked. You've got to let go, Nicole, or you'll start seeing him everywhere. Now come on. I'm starved. Let's get something to eat."

Subdued now, and doubting my instincts, I moved along with Shane. We stopped to look in shops where you could buy souvenirs or get your photo taken to be put on a magazine cover. But all the time my eyes stared not at the store window displays, but at the images of the people behind us, reflected on the glass. I held onto Shane's hand, not wanting to let go.

"How about a great cheeseburger at Mel's Diner?" he asked, smiling down at me.

"Shane? Please don't get angry with me, but I have to ask you something. Did you tell Michael you'd be here today? Did you?"

"There we go, talking about *him* again! Of course I didn't! Why would I?"

"Are you sure?"

"Yes!"

We walked along awhile, silent, a tension between us, and then Shane suddenly said, "Wait!" His face turned pink. "He asked me if I wanted to play tennis with him today!"

"And?"

"I told him. I said, 'I can't. I'm sorry. I've got tickets to Universal Studios!' "

CHAPTER
11

WHO SHOULD I talk to about Michael? I wondered. I ruled out Mom and I didn't want to worry Dad. Evie thought Michael was too nice a guy to do all the crazy things I said he was doing. Shane had to be sick of the subject. I didn't really know the school psychologist, and wasn't comfortable seeing the guidance counselor. What should I do?

Monday morning Evie and I took the shortcut that led to the back of the high school, past the tennis courts and the parking lot. I found myself glancing over my shoulder, scanning the cars.

"There he is now," Evie said, seeing Michael first. "Just ahead. Getting out of his car!"

"Did he see us?" I grabbed Evie's hand and pulled her between two cars.

"I don't know."

I slunk down and squinted through the dirty windows of a Ford Escort. Opposite us and a little closer to school Michael leaned over the trunk of his car. Rearranging things? Or waiting for me?

"You can't escape him forever, Nicole. Let's go," Evie said.

"Wait till he leaves. I can't!"

"Yes you can." She tugged at my arm. "Be civil. You *know* he wouldn't hurt you! You probably imagined you saw him yesterday. After all, he never came out of the *Star Trek* building, right? You didn't see him for the rest of the day, right?"

"He was there. I don't care what you say. Whose side are you on?"

"Be fair, Nicole. I'm on your side, of course. You don't have to say much. Just don't encourage him. You know—be friendly, that's all."

No way did I want to talk to Michael, but I left my hiding place and reluctantly joined Evie right up to and past Michael's car.

"Hi Evie. Nicole!" Michael slammed the trunk of his car shut, slung his books over one shoulder, and caught up with us. He fell in step beside me just as he had every day we'd driven to school together. Red lines blurred the whites of his eyes.

"Nicole. I've got to talk to you."

"I'll run along then. See you guys later," Evie said.

"Evie, no!"

"Remember what I told you!" Evie called, taking off. I walked as far from Michael as I could so as not to bump into him even accidentally. "What did you want to say, Michael?" I asked.

"I want to apologize." Michael spoke softly so kids passing might not hear. I hoped Shane wouldn't be near, seeing us together.

"I seem to be constantly apologizing lately, to you, to my father. . . . Dad really lit into me when I got home Sunday. He told me about your phone calls and that he didn't like being awakened at almost one o'clock in the morning by hysterical people."

"Hysterical people?! Wouldn't you be a little hysterical under the circumstances?"

Michael shrugged. "Dad asked if what you said was true—you know, that I might do myself in?"

"And?" I prodded, when he didn't go on. "You said?"

"I said . . ." He glanced anxiously at me. "I said, of course I hadn't said that. You must have misunderstood."

"In other words, you made a liar out of me. Thanks a lot!"

"Nicole, I had no choice! My father would have called me a fool! He'd have ranted on and on about keeping my eye on the ball—that no woman should ever come between me and my 'primary goal.' He'd have grounded me, forbidden me to ever talk to you again. . . . Sent me to a shrink! Forced me to transfer to an all-male school. Who knows? I just couldn't!"

I shifted the books in my arms, knowing he was probably right. Somehow I still felt sorry for him, because he had such an unpleasant father. It made me feel less belligerent. "Michael, you can't keep scaring me like that, threatening like that . . . it's not fair."

"Would you rather I just—*did* it?"

"You're doing it again! Stop it! Michael, you need help!"

"No!" He threw the words at me. "The only help I need is getting your friendship back, having your respect and attention again. That's all I need."

We'd reached the north courtyard, where kids bring their lunches to eat at the tables on nice days. This was the place where we usually separated, each going to our own homeroom classes.

"What can I say, Michael?" I clutched my books to my chest like a shield and looked up into his eyes. "I'm here if you need me, as your *friend*, that's all. I'll always be. But not if you hound me and follow me and make—threats!"

"I won't. I didn't. . . . I swear!" He looked distraught. "Can't we be friends the way we used to—you know, doing homework together and stuff? I miss it—the warmth, your family, everything. . . ."

"Listen, we can try again," I said, figuring I'd just limit how often he came over. "But the next time you threaten to hurt yourself, Michael, that's it. I can't . . . I can't be responsible for—for *your* life!" I felt tears well up and I could hardly control myself. Showing this kind of feeling was just what Evie warned against.

"You still care." Michael's eyes smiled lovingly. "You do love me; I don't care what you say!" He touched a finger to my cheek.

"Michael!" I shook my head to get away from his touch.

"It's okay, Nicole. We'll work it out one way or another. I'll be better." He walked off, whistling, and I stood there, watching him go, wanting to yell after him, "I *don't* love you! I don't!"

In the next weeks, while I continued to date Shane, I tried to show friendship to Michael. He came over one afternoon a week to study with me.

He'd stopped seeing Beth, or she'd broken up with him. I'd seen him with other girls—Kathy, Jennifer, and Coralee at lunch, and he said he was taking Anne out. I made sure not to flirt with him. I did not want to do anything to lead him on. We'd reached some kind of understanding, some kind of real friendship that had nothing to do with dating or going steady. I began to really think he'd find someone else and would lose all interest in me.

Then one afternoon, after we'd studied together in the living room and helped Melanie make oatmeal cookies, he gave me an odd smile before he left. I didn't think much about it until Mom came into the room. "What's this?" She held up an envelope. "It was on the couch. It's got your name on it." She held it out to me.

My face grew hot when I recognized Michael's writing. Why was he leaving me notes when he could say whatever he wanted to say directly?

"Aren't you going to open it?"

Without answering, I ripped open the envelope and

pulled out the folded sheet of paper. Silently, I read the message. "You are in my heart every minute of the day and night." There was much more, terribly mushy and embarrassing. All the blood in my body rushed to my head. "Grrr!" I cried, and tore the sheet into smaller and smaller pieces.

"Nicole! What's wrong? What does it say?" Mom asked.

"It's from *Michael*! He just *won't* give up! And I'm tired of it."

CHAPTER

12

I SAID NOTHING to Michael in response to his note. Instead, I began avoiding him. Being "just friends" didn't work. I should have known! He was just manipulating me again.

When he suggested coming to the house I said, "Not this week." When he phoned, I told whoever answered to say I wasn't in. If we did talk, I kept it short.

"What did I do now?" he demanded on the phone.

"Nothing. I just have other plans."

"It's because of the note, isn't it?"

"I'm very busy, that's all. I'm working. I've got school. I'm busy with other friends."

"Like *Shane*."

"Yes, like Shane!"

The next week he started coming to the library on the nights I worked. My heart stopped when I saw him the first time. Was he there to study, or to watch me? He sat at a table toward the back of the library and appeared to be very busy with his work. I went about my job, sorting and returning books to the shelves, constantly aware of his presence, but staying as far away as possible. Now and then I'd glance his way to see if he was watching.

He wasn't.

When he made no effort to talk with me I began to relax, hoping he'd go home before closing time so he wouldn't run into Shane. At ten minutes to closing I had a whole cart of children's books to put away and was rushing to get them all shelved in time, when a hand touched my back.

"Oh!" I exclaimed, swinging around, shocked out of my concentration.

"Didn't mean to scare you, Nicole. Just wondered if you want a ride home," Michael said.

"Oh! Oh, thanks. No!"

Between us lay the unspoken words, that I refused because Shane would be by or that I'd rather go home alone than with him.

He smiled. "Okay. See you tomorrow, then. S'long."

I let out my breath as he walked toward the door, and I returned to my work.

The second time that week he behaved the same, kept his nose in the books until almost closing, waved a good-bye, then left.

On Thursday evening, the night Shane always worked until ten, the library emptied by a few minutes past nine. I spent the next minutes picking up magazines and books left on tables and pushing the chairs into place. When I reached the table where Michael had sat I picked up the book he'd been reading, an encyclopedia on tennis. Typical, I thought, and stacked it on the book cart when I saw something white sticking out between the pages.

Leave it, some instinct warned, but then I thought, Maybe it's important to Michael. I slipped it out and saw my name on it.

No, I wouldn't read it! I crumpled the paper into a ball and shoved it into my pocket, then rolled the cart into the back. The library aides would put these books back in the morning.

"Your dad coming for you tonight, Nicole?" Mrs. Cohen, the librarian, asked when I got ready to leave. "Or that nice young man?"

"Shane's working tonight. I'm meeting him at the Sport Chalet and he'll drive me home." How strangely happy it made me to even mention his name.

"It's dark out. If you wait a few minutes I'll drop you," Mrs. Cohen said.

"Oh, no; that's okay. I've done it lots of times. Don't worry." I got my purse and jacket and went to the library door, dropping Michael's note in the wastebasket on the way. Mrs. Cohen unlocked the door to let me out, and then relocked it behind me.

Outside, the parking lot was already empty except for a few cars in the back, where the staff always parked. The air felt heavy and clouds hid the moon. I zipped my jacket and pulled it close at the neck, looked to the right and then to the left, and took off at a brisk pace. I wanted to get to the light and warmth of the Sport Chalet to browse near Shane until the store closed. I liked watching him work; I liked when he'd look around, between customers, and smile when he saw me nearby.

Thinking these things, I started down the dimly lit walk to the street, hearing my own steps slapping the pavement. Suddenly, I heard another sound, someone moving behind me. A shiver ran down my back. A minute ago, when I'd left the library, there'd been no one around; the parking lot was empty. If someone had left after me—a librarian—she or he would be driving! Who else would be here this time of night? Michael? No. He'd left half an hour ago!

I quickened my step and glanced back to see a dark figure hurrying toward me. Run, my head commanded. Run! Get to where people driving by might see you if someone tries to attack! Perspiration ran down my neck. My heart pumped off the scale. Why hadn't I listened to Mrs. Cohen? Oh God, I prayed, Save me!

"Wait! Nicole!"

Oh God! It was Michael! Gasping, I bent over, hands on my knees, on the verge of throwing up.

"Hey, why are you running like that?" Michael asked, catching up. "Didn't you see me? It's so dark out. I thought I'd wait and see if you wanted a ride!"

"Geez, Michael! You scared me half to death!" I cried.

"I did? Sorry! I didn't mean to. So, what do you say? Drive you home?"

I straightened up, my heart slowly returning to normal. "You shouldn't have waited. I'm meeting Shane at the Sport Chalet."

"Cowboy," he said irritably. "What do you see in him? What kind of guy lets you run around late at night, unprotected?"

"He didn't *let* me. I'm perfectly capable of walking three blocks by myself!" I dug my hands into my pockets and moved on again. Michael slid one arm through mine.

"Don't!" I drew away.

"Did you find my note?"

"Yes!"

"Did you read it?"

"No! And please stop leaving notes around for me! If you have something to say—say it!"

"Okay. I asked if you'd go to the prom with me."

"You what? The prom? You're *kidding*!" I stopped short, just under the street lamp, so I could see Michael's face. "You're not—serious?"

"Of course I am! Why wouldn't I be?"

"I don't believe this!"

"What? What don't you believe?"

"You know I can't go to the prom with you! I told you! It's not like that for us!"

"What do you mean?"

"You *know* what I mean. You have to. I can't believe you don't!"

"Why? Are you going with someone else? Has Texas asked you?"

"His name is *Shane*. No, he hasn't, not yet, but even if he doesn't, I won't go with you!"

"Why?" Michael's voice turned hoarse.

"Because I don't *want* to!"

That stopped him for only an instant, then he bellowed, "You know something, Nicole? You're a bitch! A real bitch! That's what you are! You're a lying, cheating flirt, and a tease to boot, and I'm tired of your games!"

I stepped back. Tears sprang to my eyes. I hadn't led him on. I'd been up-front from the start. I'd bent over backwards to be kind. "Fine!" I shot back. "If I'm so awful, leave me alone! Stop following me and stop coming to the house and stop phoning. Leave me *alone*!"

"No! I know deep down you still love me."

"I *never* loved you!"

"That's a lie! You did and you do! This Cowboy— it's all his doing," he went on, not even listening. "If it weren't for him . . . You're going to stop this fooling around. It's going to be just like before with us! Nobody drops me like I don't count; nobody embarrasses me with my friends. No!"

"Michael!"

He waved my objection away. "You're not going to the prom with Cowboy or anyone else! You're going with me! Understand?" He tried to take my hand, but I resisted. "You're going with *me*!"

"No! I won't! Leave me *alone*, Michael!" I jerked away from him and started running down the block. "Leave me alone!"

"Nicole!" He chased after me and grabbed my shoulder. "Wait!"

"Let go, or I'll *scream*! Let—go!"

He must have believed me, because he dropped his hand and stood still, staring at me in the dim street-light. In a totally different tone, full of regret and confusion, he started muttering. "I don't know what gets into me. You just drive me crazy! I can't think straight when you reject me like this! I'm sorry! I'm sorry. I didn't mean what I said! Don't leave me. I need you. I didn't mean any harm."

"Sure. . . ." I threw at him. "Oh, sure!" I was sick of his demands and excuses and apologies. I just wanted to get away from him, to not ever see him again. I turned on my heels and started running, away from Michael, away from *Michael*—toward the lights of the Sport Chalet. I didn't feel sorry for him anymore. I didn't even like him anymore. His spying and his nasty outbursts really scared me now.

I must have looked terrible, hair wild, face streaked with tears and perspiration, legs almost ready to buckle, when I reached the Chalet and ran inside. Light flooded the big, cheerful store. I leaned my head against the cool glass of the window to catch my breath, then jumped away as I imagined Michael outside in the dark, watching.

"You okay, Nicole?" a clerk at the checkout asked as I went by. "You look funny."

Dry mouthed, I shook my head and rushed through the aisles looking for Shane.

I found him talking to another clerk as they put shoes back on the display racks.

"Shane . . ."

He swung around. "Nicole! Nicole, what's wrong?" He took my hand. "Be right back," he told the other clerk and led me to a chair. "Do you want a drink? Are you sick? What's wrong?"

"Water, just water," I said. "I'll be okay in a minute."

Shane hurried off and in a moment returned with a paper cup of water. He watched me anxiously as I drank it down in one gulp. He glanced up when the announcement came over the loudspeaker that the store would close in ten minutes. "I've got to finish up. Will you be okay?"

"Yes, sure. Go ahead." I nodded and tried to smile.

With a backward glance of concern, he returned to his work, looking up frequently to check on me.

Calmer now, I went over in my head what had happened and what had been said. Maybe I'd been too harsh after all. Had I overreacted? Maybe I had to accept some blame. Michael hadn't meant to scare me when he followed me in the parking lot. Actually, he showed real concern in wanting to drive me home.

But what about the accusations, his outrage? What of them? Did he really think I'd led him on? I hadn't. But did I have to hurt his pride by being so incredulous about his invitation to the prom? Of course that would inflame him. It would infuriate anyone! Why hadn't I been more sensitive, kinder, and said—said, *what*? Maybe my mother was right about not giving the bitter truth to someone who couldn't easily take it.

"Hi. Let's go." Shane took my arm and we left the building for the parking lot.

"S'long, Shane. Nicole," another employee called to us. I nodded, but my eyes were elsewhere, scouring the parking lot for signs of a red Mustang, signs of Michael loitering.

"You sure you're okay?" Shane unlocked the VW door on my side.

"Now I am." I checked the backseat before sitting down and locked the door beside me. Shane went around the car and got into the driver's seat, then turned around. "Okay, now tell me—what happened?"

I thought for only two seconds before I decided to tell him everything. "He hates you, Shane. He blames everything on you. Sometimes I think he'd do something crazy, like hurt you, just to get you out of the way."

"Ah, no, Nicole. He wouldn't. Anyway, I can take care of myself. People say lots of things when they're angry. It's you I worry about. What about hurting *you*?"

"No." I shook my head. "Michael wouldn't hurt me. At least, I don't think he would."

"It's time to make a clean break. Stay away from him. He'll never get over you if he thinks he still has a chance."

"You're right. But what if he calls? What if he threatens suicide again?"

"You can't hold his hand forever. You're not responsible for him."

"But what if . . ." Suddenly I had the awful thought that it really was my fault, because I loved all the flattery and attention. Maybe I didn't really want him to stop, because of my ego. If that was so, I *was* to blame. But I *hadn't* led him on! I hadn't! I'd been honest with him. I wasn't a tease!

The light from cars leaving the parking lot brightened the cabin for an instant. Shane held my hand, studying me. "Look, Nicole. Michael's the one with the problem, not you. I promise we'll stop his fantasies. There's one way to do that. Go to the prom with *me*. Okay?"

I should have felt elated—my dream was coming true. "But what about—what he said? His threats?"

Shane put two fingers over my lips. "He was angry. He'll get over it. The prom's still two months off. By then he'll probably be madly in love with someone else.

I looked up into Shane's eyes and wanted to believe him. He was kind and intelligent. He understood people. "You think so? Really?"

"Absolutely." He leaned over and kissed me. "What do you say? I didn't hear a yes, yet. You do want to go to the prom with me, don't you? Or should I ask someone else?"

"You dare!" I cried. And then I kissed him back.

CHAPTER

13

S HANE SHOWED ME the prom announcement, which came out the very next week. First there'd be dinner and dancing at a hotel, then buses would take us to Marina del Rey, where we'd board a ferry for more dancing, a harbor cruise, and a breakfast.

"Oooh," I crooned, rapturously. "It's going to be so romantic! So wonderful!" I gazed up at him, so glad that it was he I'd be going with. It was so incredible that I'd be at a junior prom. Then I glanced further down and noticed the cost. "Oh, no! It's a fortune!"

"A small fortune, but it's worth it. It will be very special, because I'll be going with someone I really want to be with!"

My throat tightened and I leaned my face against his shoulder for an instant.

* * *

Everywhere at school the next few days people were talking about the prom. Are you going? Have you been asked? Who are you going to ask?

I wondered who Michael would ask—and then told myself to forget it; that was no longer my concern. After the library outburst I wanted nothing more to do with him. I went out of my way to avoid him, even eating lunch outdoors so he wouldn't see me.

One day, about a week after the prom announcement, Beth caught up to me as I headed home from school. Surprised that she'd want to talk to me after what happened in the restaurant, I greeted her with some uncertainty.

"Mind if I walk with you awhile?" she asked.

"Sure. What's up?"

"I was really naive, saying what I did that night at the restaurant."

"Oh, it's okay. You had a right to be angry." Something in her tone put me on guard, and she wouldn't look at me as she spoke, either.

"You don't understand. You were right. Michael was *using* me to be near you."

"I don't think he really meant to—"

Her voice rose. "Sure you'd defend him! You're pretty shrewd, Nicole, the way you engineered getting him back!"

"Huh?" I stopped walking and swung around to face her. "What are you talking about?"

"Don't play the innocent. It's very obvious. Michael wanted to break up with you and you used Shane to make him jealous! Poor Shane!"

"What?" My neck prickled.

"Sure. Don't tell me it's not true. Michael wouldn't lie, and it's all over school."

"*What?* For heaven's sake, Beth, *what's* all over school? What are you talking about?"

"You should know! You and Michael. You think he'd have asked you to the prom if you hadn't made him jealous? Congratulations. You got what you wanted. You're going with Michael. Is Shane still talking to you?"

I cut her short. "Going with Michael, to the prom? Where did you get that idea? It's not true! I'm going with Shane!"

Beth rocked back on her heels, my words sinking in slowly. "What are you talking about?" It's as if nothing I could have said would have surprised her more. Slowly her disbelief changed to puzzlement. "I don't get it. You're not? But—everyone knows . . . Who'd have . . . Michael?"

"Yes, *Michael!*"

"I don't get it!" Beth said again. "Why?"

"Who knows! I give up trying to figure him out. He thinks he can make something come true just by saying it!" We stood facing each other in the middle of the street. A man pushing a baby stroller approached, and I stepped back.

"I'm sorry. I really believed it. I'm so embarrassed," Beth said.

Her accusation still stung. How many other kids at school thought I could be so two-faced? "That's okay," I said, sadly. "But please, do me a favor. If you hear this from anyone else, please straighten them out. I am *not* going to the prom with Michael!" My eye began to twitch, and I pressed a finger over it. It was hopeless. Each time I thought I was through with Michael something new happened. What next? I bit my lip, thinking. Someone would know how to convince him to leave me alone. I had to get help somewhere. But where?

I sat in the outer office the next week, waiting for my appointment with Mrs. Sanchez, the school counselor. Hands folded tightly in my lap I continued to wrestle with myself. Evie couldn't help, and Shane couldn't, either. I needed an adult, but not one of my parents. From Mom's viewpoint, Michael could do no wrong. Dad might overreact—march over to Michael's house and talk to his father—and that would be trouble.

Mrs. Sanchez seemed the only answer. But how could I explain everything without it sounding weird? What could she possibly do about it?

Around me phones rang, computers clicked, clerks dealt with students—and I fidgeted, eyeing the clock. If Mrs. Sanchez didn't come out in two more minutes, I'd leave.

I was just gathering up my books and purse when she came out of her office and called my name.

"Sorry to keep you waiting," she said as I stood up. "Won't you come in now?" A large woman with dark hair and glasses, Mrs. Sanchez led the way to a small, crowded office and nodded to the chair she wanted me to take. She settled in behind her desk, clasped her hands, and leaned forward. "Well, Nicole. Now, what can I do for you? Is this about your program for next year?"

"No. It's about a problem I'm having with a boy I know. I hoped you could understand. "I'm afraid to discuss this with my parents. Maybe you can tell me what to do," I said.

"Tell me about it."

I told her about Michael and our friendship from the very beginning. I explained how things had changed when I met Shane. I decided to tell all, so she'd believe me, and told her about the suicide threat, about his following me, about his bullheaded notion that I loved him, when I swore I didn't. About his threat to Shane and his fantasy that I'd be going to the prom with him.

She listened without interrupting and finally said, "You'll have to tell me Michael's last name, Nicole. We have plenty of Michaels."

"Michael Donaldson."

"Oh, he's a senior. Yes, I know him."

Something in the way she said it made me think Mrs. Sanchez knew something about Michael. Maybe even things that would allow her to believe me.

"He has problems with his father," I added. "Mr. Donaldson's very demanding."

"Yes, I know," Mrs. Sanchez said.

"Then maybe you know that Mr. Donaldson taught Michael to believe that anything he sets his mind to do he can, if he tries hard enough. It may work at tennis, but it won't make me love him, no matter how hard he tries. I told him that, but he won't believe it.

"I understand," Mrs. Sanchez said. "It sounds like he's having a very difficult time accepting your breakup. I'll have a talk with him."

"Oh yes! If you could make him see that the harder he tries, the *less* I like him . . . I need someone to tell him to stay away from me, an adult, like you." My voice cracked. "And to stay away from Shane too!"

"I'll try. And Nicole, stay away from him. You only encourage him by trying to remain his friend."

"Thanks." I nodded gratitude and stared at the notebook on my lap with its ink-drawn names of my friends and the big heart with Shane's name inside. I'd never written *Michael* on my notebook cover.

"One other thing," I said, sensing Mrs. Sanchez believed me. "I don't know much about suicide. I mean, I've never known anyone who did it so I need to ask you. Does Michael mean it when he talks about killing himself or is he saying it just for attention? Is he doing it to keep me connected to him?" I pressed my hand against my chest to quiet the ache inside.

"A suicide threat is always something to take seriously," Mrs. Sanchez said. "Michael is an intense young man. We don't know if his threat is serious, but I'm certainly not willing to risk that he's bluffing. I'll call him in, Nicole, and have a talk with him. The behavior you've described is bad for him and for you. It has got to stop. If he doesn't agree, I'll call in his parents."

I let out my breath in relief "Mrs. Sanchez? I wasn't

sure I should come. I couldn't imagine anyone could help. Thanks. Thanks a lot."

Mrs. Sanchez stood up and came around the desk to put a hand on my shoulder. "Now, don't you worry. I'm sure everything will work out just fine. If Michael gives you any more trouble after I've talked to him be sure to let me know."

I felt so good as I came out of the counseling office. I was eager to find Shane and tell him *the news*. We could forget about Michael bothering us anymore. Mrs. Sanchez would fix everything. I should have thought to get help before.

CHAPTER
14

TWO DAYS LATER Michael's red Mustang sat at the curb in front of my house when I came out to go to school. He leaned against the hood, arms crossed, waiting for me.

Heart in mouth, I stopped, then swung around to go back inside.

"Nicole! Be a good sport!" he called out. "I just want to say something, then I'll never bother you again."

"Say it from there!" I shot back.

"Oh, come on! I'm not going to hurt you! Give me a chance!"

I approached slowly, then waited, close enough so he wouldn't have to shout, but far enough so I could run if I had to. "What?"

He smiled, sadly. "What's happened between us that you should be so cold?"

"You had something to tell me?"

"You shouldn't have gone to Sanchez, Nicole. That wasn't fair. You could have caused all sorts of trouble with my dad!"

"If that's all you want to say, good-bye!"

"Wait!" He lunged forward, then stopped himself a foot or two away and held up both hands in surrender. "Sanchez said I should apologize, so I'm apologizing. I'm sorry. I'm sorry! I didn't mean to scare you."

"You told everyone we were going to the prom! It was a lie! How could you?" Behind me I heard the whine of the garage door lifting, and then the sound of Dad's car starting. I glanced back, uneasy at Dad's leaving.

"I didn't mean to lie. I can't explain. It's just that— with our history together . . . I couldn't believe . . . I always figured . . ."

I stood like a statue, listening to his disjointed talk, not able to feel anything like pity or regret.

"Don't hate me, Nicole. I couldn't stand that," Michael said, picking up on my mood. "I'll stop bothering you, if that's what you want. As much as it hurts, I'll stay away."

"That's what I want."

"Okay." He gazed at me, then looked away. "Drive you to school? No. Of *course* not!" He slapped his face and grinned at his mistake. "Your *birthday's* coming up next week. Can I—"

"*No,* Michael!"

The smile faded. "Yeah. Well. See you around, then." He climbed into his car and took off with a squeal of rubber. I heaved a deep sigh and wiped my hands on my jeans, then started down the street to school.

A week later, as I waited for Shane and Evie to arrive to help celebrate my sixteenth birthday, I thought of last year. I'd only known Michael a few months, but when my birthday came he overwhelmed me with attention. He sent flowers. He took me to dinner at a restaurant even my parents thought was expensive. He gave me tapes of my favorite groups. And when I went to school that day, he'd managed to get a message on the announcement board reading: HAPPY BIRTHDAY, NICOLE!

I'd been excited and flattered and awed.

This, my sixteenth birthday, would be much different. Months ago Mom had offered to make a special party for me and my friends, but I'd turned her down.

"If you don't want a party, what would you like?" she'd asked.

"Just a few of my favorite people—Evie and Shane and Louise and Norman—and my own family at dinner. And—if it's not outrageously expensive—a really good telescope."

She'd see what she could do, she said.

Shane arrived first. When I opened the door he bent forward and kissed me, hands behind his back. Then, he handed me a bouquet of purple irises and yellow daisies. They were beautiful, but I found myself thinking, Is that all?

"Happy birthday. Feel any older? You look at least a day older than yesterday." He put an arm around my waist and came inside. The bell rang again and there were Louise and Norman, and behind them, Evie.

Mom made all my favorite foods, with a fabulous double-chocolate cake for dessert. I can't even remember what we all talked about, but everyone laughed a lot and by the time dinner ended I felt warm and wonderfully happy.

Ribboned boxes and greeting cards covered the top of the buffet. Melanie brought them one by one to the table when it was time to open presents.

"Mine first!" she exclaimed, hanging over me as I unwrapped her gift. It was a box of pink stationery with my name imprinted on the paper and envelopes.

"Just what I wanted!" I exclaimed, giving my sister a big hug.

Louise and Norman gave me a beautiful wooden jewel box with a mirror under the lid, a tray for earrings and pins, and a lower section for necklaces. Evie bought me a teddy, white and satiny soft and as light as a rose petal! Holding it up for everyone to see I glanced at Shane and blushed.

"And what's this?" I asked, as if I didn't know, when Mom and Dad's gift was passed to me. I tore at the pretty wrapping on the big box, then clawed at the heavy staples sealing the brown cardboard until Dad handed me a screwdriver. Inside was more packing, of Styrofoam. At last, with a sense of reverence, I lifted out the telescope.

"Ooooh!" I ran my hand down the cool brass finish of the tube. "Just look at it! And what magnification!

I'll be able to see everything!" I could feel the love and gratitude pouring out of my eyes as I looked at my parents. "It's the best present you could possibly have given me!"

"And this may be useful, too." Shane reached under his chair and handed me another package. "Happy birthday."

"What? But you already gave me . . ." I dropped the telescope instruction booklet back in the box and took his present. "What's in here, lead?" I teased.

"Rocks," Shane said. "Open it."

I slid a nail under the Scotch tape and carefully folded the wrapping back. It was a book on the heavens—beautifully illustrated with dozens of color plates that would be a pleasure to browse through and totally helpful when using the telescope. I almost cried. Every gift had been thoughtful and perfect.

While Mom poured second cups of tea and coffee everyone chatted away. I made my way through the pile of birthday greetings that Mom had set aside for me to open at the party. There were cards from friends at school, from aunts, uncles, and Grandma and Grandpa. I was even glad to get some with checks inside!

"Here's one without anything on it." Shane passed an envelope to me. "Must have been delivered by hand."

I immediately felt anxious. *Michael!* Who else? Had he managed to invade this special day?

With distaste I ripped the envelope open and pulled out the card. The cover showed a little bear, and the message read: "Do I ever think of you? Nah . . ." I opened it up and inside it said: "Except—in the morning; when the sun's out; before I go to sleep; in the spring; when it's raining; after lunch . . . Happy sixteenth! Always, Shane."

"Shane! Oh! It's *yours*!" I cried with relief.

"Whose did you think it was? Oh. . . ." he added, when he realized.

"I guess I just still feel anxious about him," I whispered to Shane. "I half expected him to show up and spoil everything. Mrs. Sanchez must have gotten through to him." I squeezed Shane's hand under the table. "Thanks. Everything is wonderful—the card, the flowers, and the book."

We grinned at each other until I caught Norman watching. He smiled. I felt a bit flustered. "Shane's going to help me set up the telescope," I said, and we excused ourselves and went to the other room.

The prom was coming up in only a few weeks. I kept worrying about what to wear. It was good to have a problem like that! Even though Evie wasn't invited, she wanted to help me find the perfect dress. I was glad that she was excited for me, and I almost forgot about Michael. Maybe that was because he seemed to have given up after our last talk, just before my birthday. I began to feel secure, freed from his web.

One Saturday, while Shane worked, Evie and I went to every store in the mall to search for my dress. Evie pretended to be looking for a dress too, so we both tried things on. She'd select dramatic, flowing outfits that made her look even more like a model out of *Vogue*. My taste ran as usual, to conservative-styled gowns.

"You looked best in the white dress," Evie said as we left the mall without anything. "Buy the white one, and then you could borrow my white beaded bag. With flowers in your hair and white satin shoes, you'd be smashing!" She hopped on one foot and adjusted the Band-aid on her heel, grimacing. "I promise I'll do your makeup. Get your mom to spring for the white."

"Forget it! Did you see the price on that dress?"

"Then how about the strapless black one?"

"For you, maybe. I look like the Wicked Witch of the West in black." My eye caught a flash of red at the curb, and my heart turned over.

"Is that Michael's car just ahead?" Evie asked, before I said a word.

"Yes! Hurry!" I grabbed Evie's arm and swung around. "If we go the other way we can get to the bus stop without him seeing us."

"Come *on*, Nicole!" Evie cried, pulling her arm free and stopping in her tracks. "That's eight blocks out of the way, my heel's killing me, and my date is coming over in an hour! Besides, Michael's probably not even in the car! Stop being so paranoid! He hasn't bothered you in weeks."

"I'm not paranoid!"

"Honestly! I talk to Michael at school all the time. He's dating Beth again. He's taking her to the prom. I told you that. Don't make him into some kind of monster."

He was like a monster to me, but I just nodded and kept walking away from the car, in the direction of the bus stop. Evie followed me all the while, griping about how much her heel hurt. Three blocks into our walk Michael pulled up alongside us.

"Hey! Want a lift?" He smiled disarmingly and slowed to match our pace.

"No thanks!" I returned.

Evie whispered, "Nicole! The bus takes half an hour! Michael could have us home in ten minutes!"

"You go with him, then!"

"What do you say, girls? Make up your minds!"

"I'm going!" Evie cried. "You want to take the bus, fine! Thanks, Michael!" she called out, limping over to the car. "You saved my life."

"Nicole?"

I hesitated.

"Oh come on, Nic!" Evie said. "It'll be so much quicker."

"Oh—all right!" I climbed into the backseat, leaving Evie to sit beside Michael. What could happen with her there?

"How'd you do at the tennis tournament last week?" Evie asked, making conversation as we drove. "I hear your brother's doing real well, too." She chattered on and I caught her last words. "Evan told me you're going to the prom with Beth."

I gazed out the window, eager to get home. They were ignoring me. Michael pulled up in front of Evie's house. She thanked him, waved good-bye to me, and got out. I pushed back the front seat and hurried to follow her.

"Where you going, Nicole?" Michael asked. "It's only a half mile. I'll take you to your door."

"That's all right."

"It's not all right! You act like I'm a serial killer or something! Stay put; I'll have you home in two seconds!"

"Promise?"

"I promise. Now get back in!"

I settled in the front seat beside Michael, figuring that way I could get out quickly if I had to. He drove off slowly, humming a Beatles song. "So, how's it going?" he asked after a while. "I wanted to send you something for your birthday, but the way you take things lately, I figured I shouldn't. Have a party?"

"Just the family."

"*Evie* was there, too. And *Shane*."

"Yes, Evie and Shane. How did *you* know?"

"Hah!" He laughed, humorlessly. "I know everything."

"Really!" I clenched my fists and huddled close to the car door. Better not get him angry or upset. I tried for something impersonal. "Congratulations on that win last week. Think you'll get the state trophy?"

Michael took his eyes off the road and grinned at me. He must have been encouraged by my comment, because he reached over and tried to put an arm around my shoulders.

"Don't!" I grabbed his hand and pulled his arm away.

"Do—don't! I don't get you! One minute you run hot, the next cold! I bet you're not that way with *Shane*!" he jeered. "You two *doing* it?"

"What?" When his nasty question registered, I screamed, "Stop! Let me out right here!"

"Stop, Let me out right here!!" Michael mocked. Instead of stopping, he picked up speed and headed, not toward my house, but up into the hills.

"Michael! You promised to take me home! Slow down, you're scaring me!" My throat felt tight and my hands got sweaty. He ran a red light and picked up speed. "Stop! Please! You'll kill us both!"

"Good! We'll die together!"

"Slow down. Please! Oh Michael, *please!*" The speedometer read over seventy and was rising.

I grabbed for the ignition key.

In one swift movement Michael's right hand clamped down on mine. "Let go or I'll kill us both, right now," he warned. "See that tree ahead?" He floored the accelerator, leaned forward and with jaw set and eyes narrowed, headed straight for it.

I screamed and pressed my hands over my eyes.

"Fooled you!" Michael exclaimed gleefully. We bounced hard over a speed bump and raced on through stop signs and red lights. I forced my back against the seat, braked with my feet, and focused on the onrushing road, not daring to blink. He'd kill us for sure, I thought, heart pounding. The speedometer hit eighty-five and we barely missed a skateboarder. I started to shake. I started to cry.

"Don't! Nicole, don't! I can't stand it when you cry!"

"Then slow down. Please, Michael. Slow down! Stop! Let me out!" Tears streamed down my face.

Miraculously he slowed, back to seventy and slower. As swiftly as his anger flared, it died. Apologies and excuses spilled out of him. I'd heard all this before, each time spoken with the same intense sincerity and remorse. This time I barely heard them. "What do you want me to do?" he asked, turning sorrowful eyes on me. "I'll drive you home. . . ."

"Just . . . let me out here, I'll walk."

Michael's lips set in a hard line, and for an instant I feared he would put me through that terror again. Instead, he slowed. Even before we'd come to a complete stop I opened the door, ready to scramble out.

"I'm sorry, Nicole. If only you wouldn't . . ."

I jumped from the car before he could change his mind and started running. My heart pounded in my ears and my legs nearly folded. I ran harder. Behind me I heard the car picking up speed again.

A moment later there was a squeal of tires as Michael made a fast U-turn and started back downhill.

"No, Michael; no, don't!" I prayed, glancing over my shoulder as I ran, seeing the red Mustang roaring toward me. With a last burst of strength I leaped onto the road shoulder and tried to climb the barbed wire fence. I felt a sharp jab of pain in one hand, and then the *whoosh* of air as Michael's car screamed by.

Eyes closed tightly, I clutched the wire fence until I heard the car moving farther and farther away, ca reening downhill, gaining momentum. Only then did I let go.

He's crazy, I cried to myself, wanting to throw up. More tears slid down my cheeks. I licked my bleeding palm as I ran. *He's crazy!* He's trying to kill me. What can I do? What can I do?

CHAPTER
15

"**N**ICOLE? THAT YOU?" Mom called from her study, just off the entry hall. I staggered into the house, out of breath, sweaty, legs shaking. Michael hadn't come back, hadn't tried to run me down again, as I'd feared every step of the way home. I leaned against the front door, panting. I was safe, safe at last.

"Come in here a minute, honey!" Mom called. "I finally did that interview with Shane's parents. It's nearly done. They're just lovely people! Nicole?"

I dragged myself into the study. Mom sat, back to me, at the computer. "Did you know Mrs. Richards is a librarian? And Mr. Richards graduated from Michigan just a year after your dad," she rattled on. "I'm going to have them here to dinner next week! Would you like that? Shane too, of course." She swung around, face animated, and then she saw me. "Nicole! What is it? What happened?" She pushed her chair away and rushed to my side.

I fell into her arms and clung to her, crying like a small child. "There, there," Mom said, stroking my hair and patting my back. "It's going to be all right. It's going to be all right."

I wiped my eyes with the back of my hand until Mom handed me a tissue. Then she cupped her hands around my face and forced me to look at her. "Now what is it? What's happened? Sit down and tell me!"

I'd avoided telling Mom about all the problems with Michael until now. I believed she'd only defend him, because she liked him so much. Besides, I should be old enough to handle my own problems, I thought. But now I needed to talk. I wanted someone to help me make some sense of it all. I had to find a way to deal with Michael in the future.

Mom led me to the couch and went into the kitchen to get me something to drink. "Drink. It'll do you good." My hand shook as I took the glass.

I gulped the juice thirstily and felt a little calmer. Then I told her everything that had happened between me and Michael, from the very beginning to the incident just minutes ago.

"He could have killed you! Both of you!" Mom cried. "He's unbalanced! He needs help! Why didn't you tell me before?"

I couldn't. You always defended him. I thought everything would be fine after Mrs. Sanchez talked to him, but it wasn't. He even started dating Beth again. I don't know what to do."

"This is incredible. He almost killed you. You should have told *me* this sooner. We've got to stop this. I'm going to call his mother!"

"No, Mom. She won't do a thing. His father runs the family."

"Then I'll call his father!" Mom reached for the phone. "What's the number?"

"He'll get mad if you say anything to his dad."

"Nicole," Mom answered. This is serious. Give me his number."

I rattled off Michael's home number and waited while Mom dialed. The phone rang several times. My stomach knotted at the possibility that Michael might pick it up.

"Mrs. Donaldson?" Mom said. "This is Marsha Webber, Nicole's mother. May I speak with your husband, please?"

Mrs. Donaldson must have said her husband wasn't home and asked if she could help, because Mom then added, "It's about Michael. And it's extremely important."

Mom held her hand over the mouthpiece and whispered to me that either Michael's father had been home all along or he was just coming in the door. A minute later Michael's father boomed a hello that even I could hear.

"Mr. Donaldson," Mom began. "I'm calling about Michael. Your son nearly killed my daughter this afternoon! He said he'd drive her home and instead he took off into the hills ignoring stop signs and running red lights—at eighty miles an hour! He threatened to kill himself *and* Nicole by crashing into a tree! Michael's a very troubled young man. He's been harassing Nicole for months, phoning, following her, writing notes, threatening—"

"Mrs. Webber!" Michael's father bellowed so loud Mom held the receiver away from her ear. "Hold it right there! My son is not 'troubled.' He's as normal as you or I. Your daughter is the problem, if there is one. She's a tease and a liar!"

"Mr. Donaldson!"

"It's true. I don't know what your daughter told you, but there are two sides to every story! Nicole has played my son like a fish on a line. If she didn't want anything to do with him, ask her what was she doing riding in his car? *She's* the one doing the chasing, lady. Let me tell you! The night Michael took another girl out? Maybe you didn't know—but *your* daughter phoned close to one in the morning to see if he was home yet! Claimed he threatened suicide. Don't tell me my son's at fault!"

"You haven't heard a word I said!" Mom exclaimed. "Michael needs psychological—"

"That's an insult!" Mr. Donaldson returned. "What Michael needs is for your daughter to stay out of his life! Tell her to find someone else to obsess about. If anyone needs help, it's your daughter!"

Mom gripped the phone so her knuckles turned white. Her brown eyes narrowed. "Listen to me, Mr. Donaldson. Your son nearly killed my daughter today.

That's a fact. Whether she should have gotten into his car in the first place is immaterial. He's made serious threats against her and her boyfriend. Just what are you going to do about it?"

"All right. I'll talk to Michael, hear what *he* has to say. It's my guess he'll tell me just what I expect, that your daughter is making a mountain out of a molehill. He took her for a joyride just as any kid his age might do—and she's screaming that he tried to kill her."

I shook my head vigorously when I heard what he said, and Mom pressed her lips together in irritation.

"Now, if you'll excuse me," Mr. Donaldson continued, "I don't mean to be curt, but I do have things to do. If she were my daughter I'd advise her to stop playing games with boys older than herself, and to stick closer to the truth!"

Mom held the buzzing phone for an instant, then slammed the receiver down. "I have never, never in my whole life, spoken to anyone so unpleasant. He's completely closed-minded and defensive. He's in complete denial!"

"Mom? What are we going to do? I used to feel sorry for Michael, but now I just feel he's as stubborn as his father."

"We'll give him a chance to talk with Michael, first. If that doesn't work—I'll go the principal and the counselor. We've got to get through to Michael that this behavior has got to stop. Maybe we'll have to have someone outside of his family get him psychological help.

"Meanwhile, his father's right about one thing. You

shouldn't have gotten into the car, Evie or no Evie. From all you've said, you should know just how unpredictable he is. You just can't trust what he might do next."

"But Mom!" I protested, angry that I had to take any blame.

"No buts!" Mom noticed the blood on my hand for the first time. She took my hand in hers and gently removed the tissue I'd pressed against the puncture. "That looks bad. When did you have your last tetanus shot?"

I waved Mom's concern away. "But Mom, Michael's made threats about the prom—about my going with Shane!"

"Come in the bathroom and let's get some disinfectant." We both stood up. "I wouldn't worry. What Michael needs is a good strong authority figure, stronger than his dad, to put the fear of God in him. If his father doesn't straighten him out, I'll see to it that the principal does! Meanwhile, stay away from him—*completely*. Don't talk to him! Don't answer if he asks you anything. Don't defend yourself if he tries to insult you. Just *walk away*! He'll get the message."

"Do you really think so?" I asked hopefully.

"Yes," Mom said with certainty. "I do."

CHAPTER
16

"WHAT?" SHANE CRIED when I told him what happened. I'd waited at the library after work until I could get a ride to the Sport Chalet, and rode home with him. "He could have killed you! Now he's gone too far! I'm going over there and beating the daylights out of him!"

"No, Shane, no!" I begged, anxiously checking behind us for Michael's car, but seeing only headlights. "That's not why I told you! Don't you see? He's not rational. You can't predict what he'll do next, and you have to be careful because it's you he blames for everything!"

"Shoot!" Shane's voice held nothing but contempt. "It's months since we started dating. He's a wimp. The way he's going on over losing you is ridiculous. It's not easy loving someone who doesn't feel the same, but to grovel, to beg, to threaten like that! He's lost all my respect."

I nodded. I had lost respect for Michael long ago, it seemed. Self-pity was too easy an excuse, however. Something was wrong. Michael seemed normal to everyone. He kept up his schoolwork, played terrific tennis, even dated. When I saw him with our old friends, I knew that most people wouldn't believe he'd be so weird. What went on inside his head?

I remembered reading an article about some guy who sent love letters and presents to a movie star. The star never actually received them, because her publicity people handled things like that. But one day, because she never returned his calls or letters, he found out where she lived, stood outside her house, and when she was coming out he attacked her. The attack was so vicious that she wound up in the hospital for weeks!

But *that* guy was a psycho. I was sure he had no friends, no other life except this fantasy about the actress. Michael wasn't like that. I shuddered just thinking about the whole situation.

I moved closer to Shane. The only times I felt safe these days were when I was with him.

The next day Shane stopped by my classroom to escort me to the cafeteria. "Just for a few days," he said. "Until we're sure Michael won't bother you." I didn't object; in fact, I felt grateful.

We bought our lunches and moved outdoors, as far from Michael and his table as possible. It was a clear, sunny day, the kind of day you want to skip school and just play around outdoors.

"I'm almost finished with that short story I told you about," Shane said when we settled down at one of the few empty tables. "I worked on it until two this morning!" He unwrapped a sandwich and studied it as if he didn't know what was in it. "The writing's been like climbing a mountain. Getting to the top is hard, but sliding down the back is easy. It's been tough to really know my characters. Keeping the action going and feeling as if everything is in place was a challenge. Now it's come together. The ending is practically writing itself."

I touched his arm. "When can I read it?"

"Soon. When I'm satisfied with it." He bit into his sandwich.

"Are you ready to tell me what it's about?"

"It's about a group of scientists in a minireplica of the earth . . ." Shane stopped in midsentence. He seemed to be looking beyond me and his expression changed.

"You two look cozy!" I recognized Michael's voice and felt hands on my shoulders.

"Not *you* again," Shane exclaimed. "Get lost, Donaldson. Come on, don't make a scene."

"Leave me alone, Michael!" I said, shrugging him off.

"You want a scene?" Michael grinned at Shane. "I'll give you one!" He leaped up on the bench in the space beside me and from there to the lunch-table top. Hands on hips, he shouted, "Listen up, everyone!"

The murmur of voices lowered and students at tables nearby swung around. It became so still and I heard a car alarm that no one had stopped. I tugged at Michael's jeans leg, scanning the area for the lunch-duty teacher. "Michael, come down! You'll get in trouble!"

Michael bent and roughly pushed my hand away, then straightened up and turned slowly on the table-top. "I have an announcement to make!" he called again.

I pushed away my milk carton and gazed up at him, an ominous feeling in the pit of my stomach.

Michael did a little tap dance and a few kids giggled, then he shouted, "Now, do I have your attention?" He cupped a hand to his ear, then, grinning, said, "Good! Now hear this: Nicole Webber is—a *slut*! She is a low-down, cheating bitch! And that's the truth!"

"Michael!" I gasped, horrified. Tears of betrayal, anger, and shame sprang to my eyes. I wanted to die. A boy at a table nearby whispered to his friend and pointed at me.

"You bastard!" Shane cried. He jumped up and grabbed Michael around the legs, trying to pull him down. Michael fought him off, shouting obscenities all the time, but Shane brought him to the ground and started punching him. Michael slugged back and I screamed, "Stop it! Stop it!" while kids cheered and called encouragement. Finally the lunch-duty teacher came running up.

I didn't stay to watch. Hands over my ears, eyes streaming tears, I slid off the bench and ran. I had to get away from everyone, had to hide. It would be all over school in hours. I'd never be able to show my face again.

"Leave me alone! Go away!" I cried to whoever was following me, but in a moment a hand caught my arm and Evie murmured, "It's me, Nicole. No one believes him. He didn't mean what he said; he's crazy! I'm sorry I didn't understand how bad it was before."

We went into the rest room and I splashed water over my face. "How could he do this to me?" I cried. "I never wanted to hurt him! How could he say such things? They're not true!"

Evie handed me some paper towels. "Of course they're not. Forget it. You have nothing to be ashamed of. He's gone bonkers, that's all. You said he's crazy and obviously he is. Come on, let's go back out."

The bell rang for end of first lunch. I rushed into one of the stalls and locked the door as a crowd of girls came into the rest room.

"You hear what happened outside?" one of them asked. "Michael Donaldson, the tennis champ, called a girl named Nicole all kinds of awful names!"

"I know Nicole. She's no slut. She's not any of the things he said!" Evie said. "He's weird!"

"I don't know. He went with her a long time. Maybe he knows."

"Yeah. They used to be together all the time, and now she's tight with that new guy from Texas."

"*He* sure roughed Michael up. They were both bleeding. Crawford sent them to the office!"

I sat on the toilet lid, hand over my mouth to keep

silent. The bell rang, and soon all the footsteps and water running and voices stopped. When the last girl left, Evie tapped on the door. "Come on out now, Nicole. They're gone."

"I can't! Did you hear what they said?"

"Don't be silly! You can't stay in there forever! Where will you sleep? How will you shower? What do you want me to do, bring your meals?" She suppressed a giggle. "Come on, Nicole, be real. In two minutes this place will be swarming again with second lunch students. You want to cut classes and go home? Fine. Let's go, but *now*!"

I unlocked the door and walked out. I hated Michael for making me feel dirty and vulnerable.

"Walk by these guys like nothing happened," Evie ordered, linking arms with me. We crossed the lunch yard filling with kids. "Hi!" She greeted a boy she knew, and we walked on. I turned my face away. "Nicole, quit that. Stand tall. Be proud. You did nothing wrong!"

I bit my lip and fought back tears.

"You're doing just fine. Now we turn left and go up the hill and before you know it, we'll be at your house!"

Shane phoned an hour later. "You okay, Nicole?" he asked, right away.

"Yes," I said, though discouraged and exhausted. "Evie's here. What about you?"

"A black eye is all, and a bruised fist. Michael lost a tooth. We've been suspended—three days. But some good's come of it. After Mr. Watts chewed us out about fighting in the schoolyard he called Sanchez in. I told her what happened, and about how Michael nearly ran you down yesterday."

My skin crawled at the thought that the principal and the counselor would have heard the ugly things Michael said. "Did Michael hear all this?"

"Yes."

"What did *he* say?"

"He admitted it, but claimed it was just a joke. Oh, yeah, maybe it went too far, he said, and I'll quote him, 'Shane got me mad telling me not to make a scene. All I said was "hi" and how happy they looked together. All right—*cozy*, same thing,' he added when I corrected him. 'What right did he have talking to me like that?' " Shane paused. "Michael is bonkers for sure."

I could imagine Michael with his clean-cut good looks and usual commanding manner snowing the principal and Mrs. Sanchez. "What's the good thing that came of it?" I asked, wearily.

"Sanchez told Michael she'd be calling his parents, that she wanted them to come in for a talk. You should have seen Michael. He turned white as a ghost. Now he'll have to behave himself. After that, Watts read us the riot act and said we were suspended. That's it."

Dad phoned the principal the next day. "I want that boy expelled," he bellowed over the phone. "Or transferred. I do not want him to have any chance to hurt my daughter again!"

Mr. Watts assured Dad that he was dealing with the problem, that he would be talking with Michael's parents and conferring with his counselor. "Bear with me," Mr. Watts told Dad. "Michael has been made fully aware of the seriousness of his behavior and has expressed deep regret."

"The devil with his regret!" Dad cried. "He's apologized two dozen times; much good that does! He's attacked my daughter's reputation. He's jeopardized her life! This has got to stop!"

Mr. Watts promised it would, and said he'd let us know what steps he'd taken in a few days.

Even though I returned to school I still felt uncomfortable. Michael had a lot of friends and he was very persuasive. Most of my friends had been Michael's first. Their loyalty would be to him, regardless of what they might think of what he did. Every time I passed one of them the blood rose to my face. I searched my conscience again and again for some shred of truth to Michael's accusations and came up blank each time.

Three days later Mom and I had an appointment in Mr. Watts's office.

"Mrs. Webber, Nicole." Mr. Watts greeted us, leaning across his large desk to shake Mom's hand. "I've asked Mrs. Sanchez and Michael's counselor, Mr. Karl, to join us in case you have any questions I can't answer. Please. Have a seat."

Mrs. Sanchez nodded at me and smiled. Mom and I took chairs near the counselors. Dad wanted to come too, but we assured him it would be fine without him having to miss work. I folded my hands tightly in my lap and stared at the principal.

Mr. Watts is a large man; not just tall but big, and he always wears a suit and tie, even on the hottest days. Someone said he'd been a colonel in the army, which is probably good training for running a high school.

"I called you here to reassure you about Michael Donaldson's behavior," Mr. Watts said, twirling a pencil between his fingers. "I don't believe he'll be any more trouble."

"Oh?" Mom questioned. "How can you assure us of that?"

"I spoke with his father," Mr. Karl said. I remembered Michael saying he'd liked Mr. Karl a lot.

"Did Mr. Donaldson acknowledge his son's culpability?" Mom's question held a tinge of sarcasm and disbelief.

Mr. Karl glanced first at the principal, as if wanting permission, then said, "In fact, he wasn't very cooperative."

"Then how can you assure us of anything!" Mom's voice rose.

"Well . . . actually, it was *Mrs.* Donaldson who gave us that promise. Mr. Donaldson had requested I not contact her. That her health was delicate and he didn't want to worry her. It seems she learned what happened from Michael. He was very upset and finally went to her."

Michael's mother had always struck me as a timid woman, afraid of her husband and awed by her sons.

"Mrs. Donaldson had a serious talk with Michael," Mr. Karl continued. "She came in with him yesterday.

He assured me, in front of her, that he would *never* do anything like that again. I believed him.

"He asked if he could apologize to you, personally."

"Oh, no!" I held up my hands as if to ward off a blow. "No, really!"

The principal nodded. "I'd like you to know, Nicole, that I warned Michael to stay away from you, that if I ever again heard of him bothering you he'd be expelled immediately and he could forget about graduating." Mr. Watts leaned toward me, sincere eyes probing. "Are you satisfied, Nicole? Do you feel better about all this? Have you any questions?"

"Nicole?" Mom asked.

"I don't know. Maybe. I want to believe you, but I'm still scared. He's promised before and it hasn't meant a thing. Maybe he won't do what he's already done, but that doesn't mean he won't do something else. Something worse! I wish you'd understand how I feel. I'm scared. I'm not sure he *can* control himself."

"I think Michael's mother got through to him," Mrs. Sanchez said, trying to reassure me. "Mr. Watts's threat certainly reached him, because he cares a great deal about graduating, and he'd be in real trouble with his father if expelled. We'll be watching him; all his teachers have been put on alert. I've recommended he talk to the school psychologist, but his father is against psychological intervention. We'll have to give the family a chance, though."

I shrugged and tried to appear more hopeful, but I couldn't.

"Try to put all this unpleasantness behind you," Mr.

Watts said, standing up. "I'm *sure* Michael will be no more trouble. His behavior has been totally inappropriate, but since it's out in the open now he'll have to control himself."

I nodded, and stood, too.

The principal came around the desk and put a hand on my arm. "Now, if Michael unfortunately should be a nuisance in any way, I want you to come straight to me."

"Thanks," I said. "I will."

Outside in the hall Mom said, "Since his mother got involved I think you can stop worrying. With the school involved now his father has to take this seriously. It will get better, I think. I really do."

"I hope so, Mom."

She gave me a hug. "I've got to go, honey. You have a good day. I think you don't have to be anxious anymore. See you tonight." She turned and strode away as I went to class.

I hurried down the empty hall to the stairway and up the stairs to my third-floor class. *Stop worrying,* Mom had said. Sure. I would. His mother would make Michael act reasonably. Sure.

But then I saw a shadow up ahead—footsteps coming up the stairs behind me? Oh! I reached the third floor and started to run.

Stop worrying, Mom said.

Right, but how?

CHAPTER
17

THE FIRST THING I saw when I awoke the morning of the prom was my dress. It hung on the door on a padded hanger, in a clear plastic bag. I smiled. I'd finally bought one that was white and filmy, with appliquéd flowers at the waist, a tight bodice, and a full skirt. I could hardly wait to get ready—the dress, the matching shoes, the white beaded purse Evie had loaned me.

A shiver of excitement raced through me. Sometimes I'd felt this day would never come. All week I'd wished the hours away. Last night I'd hardly slept, going over the things to do when I got back from work, all before seven o'clock when Shane was due. And then—a whole night of celebration! A whole night—with Shane!

"This is the big day, huh?" Dad said at breakfast.

He winked at me. "I bet you'll be the queen of the ball."

"Excited?" Mom asked.

"Can't you tell?" Melanie pointed at me. "Look. Her bathrobe's on backwards!"

I laughed. "I don't know why I'm so nervous. You'd think it was my wedding day!"

"That's how I felt too," Mom said, smiling at Dad, "the night you took me to the prom."

Everyone at the library knew about my date. Mrs. Cohen asked if I was having my hair done and if my boyfriend knew the color dress I'd be wearing so he could order a corsage. She told me to be sure to take pictures so they could all see how we looked.

The day dragged by endlessly. I'd thought about taking the day off, but figured that would make it seem even longer to wait. Ten minutes felt like an hour, even though I helped out during story hour and worked at the checkout desk.

Mrs. Cohen shooed me out early. "Go home and get ready for your nice young man," she said. "And have a wonderful time!"

I stood in the deserted parking lot remembering that night when Michael frightened me.

Hurry up, Mom, I thought, just as she pulled up.

"The florist delivered a *beautiful* wrist corsage for you," she said as soon as I climbed in the car. "And there was a bouquet of balloons on the front doorknob when I went out this morning! I put them in your room."

"Oh, Shane!" I cried, delighted.

"You want help getting ready?"

"Evie's coming to do my nails and my makeup and to fix my hair. Mom?" My voice must have taken on a certain edge because Mom took her eyes from the road to glance at me.

"You remember what I told you Michael said—about the prom? Do you think . . . ?"

"No, I don't! Now stop that!" she exclaimed. "Get it through your head that he's no threat anymore. You told me yourself, he hasn't even spoken to you since Mr. Watts ordered him to stay away, right? Right?" Mom repeated when I didn't answer.

"Right."

"Then believe it. Whatever he said about the prom you can just forget. You're going with Shane. Michael knows it, and he's come to accept it. You're going to the prom, and you're going to have the time of your life!"

"Oh, Nicole, you look marvelous!" Evie cried when I'd slipped into the new dress and she zipped me up in back. "Just look at yourself."

I swung around to the mirror, loving the way the skirt swirled around my legs then floated back again. I looked so—pretty! My eyes went from me to the balloons tied to the rocker near the window, and then back. I felt like the balloons looked—happy!

The dress emphasized my small waist and made me appear taller, more slender. Evie had helped with everything. She'd brushed my curly hair back and tied it with a white satin ribbon, leaving wisps that curled around my ears and forehead. She'd applied the eye makeup and a pink blush, and finished with lipstick.

"Well, what do you think?" Evie studied me in the mirror.

"Evie! I can't believe it! Is that *me*?"

"The same! Oh, dear! Don't you dare spoil it with tears!" She darted off to get the tissue box.

I dabbed carefully at my eyes with a tissue. "I only wish you were going too, Evie." I turned to hug my friend, but she held me at arm's length.

"Let's go show my work of art to your folks before Shane gets here," she said. "And then I've got to go."

Shane arrived soon after. Dad brought him to the living room where I was waiting with Evie, Mom, and Melanie. He looked so handsome in his tuxedo that I felt suddenly shy.

"Oh, my," he exclaimed when I stood up to greet him. "Oh, my, my, my!"

I gazed down at my hands, overwhelmed by his adoring look.

"Thanks for the beautiful flowers," I said, holding out my wrist for him to see. "And the balloons. . . ."

"Balloons. . . ." he repeated, still gazing at me.

"You look like movie stars!" Melanie exclaimed, holding on to Dad's arm.

"You both look beautiful, don't they, honey?" Mom asked.

"Absolutely. Now wait here just one minute! Can't let you go without recording this for posterity! Hang tight!" Dad dashed off to get his camera.

Fifteen minutes later we left the house, no longer shy with each other. Dad had snapped so many pictures that after a while I nudged Shane and crossed my eyes. He crossed his too, and we laughed.

"Okay, okay," Dad said at last. "I get the message." He packed up the camera and put it away.

Shane had borrowed his father's Buick, which was in better shape than Hi-Ho Silver. He opened the door for me and I got in carefully, gathering my skirt so it wouldn't catch in the door, then he went around to the driver's side. Just before he climbed in he pulled at something stuck under the windshield wiper and tossed it away.

"What was that?" I asked when he got in. "That thing you threw away.?"

"Nothing much. A flower; a rose, I think."

I felt the first stirrings of uneasiness. "A rose? That's strange. What's a rose doing on your car?"

"Who knows? My sister probably put it there; she likes doing nutty things like that." He turned a brilliant smile on me. "Ready for a wonderful time, Cinderella?" He leaned over, took me by the shoulders, and kissed me gently. "You smell wonderful."

I brought his face close, loving the soft way he kissed. "Again."

He gave me another kiss. "Keep this up and we'll never get to the prom!" He drew back, plugged the key in the ignition, and started the engine. He checked for oncoming cars, eased out into the street, then he said, "That's funny. Feels like a flat. Darn. I hope not!

Better have a look." He turned off the engine and left the key in the ignition.

"Shane . . . wait," I called, the uneasy feeling back, but he was already out, circling the car. I watched him through the window, bending to inspect each tire, and then climbed out, too.

"Look!" he said. "Flat! This one, and the front on your side's low, too. The valve cap's been taken. Now, that's got to be more than a coincidence! That's deliberate vandalism!"

"*Michael.*" I murmured, heart banging hard against my ribs. "He threatened to do something to stop us, Shane."

Shane's forehead puckered into a frown. He peered into the darkness. "Maybe. Maybe not. I've got a good spare. Better change the tire and pump some air in the one that's low, then get to a station and check them all." He removed his jacket and laid it across the seat. "Sorry, Nicole. I'll be as fast as I can."

"I'll get Dad. He can phone Triple A and they'll tow us."

"No. We don't have Triple A. Don't worry. Just let me do it my way. I'll have it changed in no time!" He went to the trunk and opened the lid. I hoped my family wasn't watching at the window. I looked over and didn't see anyone. Then I followed him around, eyes scanning the street on both sides. I wondered how Michael had managed to do this so fast. He could be behind any of the parked cars, or hiding in the hedge in front of the Browns' house across the street. Or in the shadow of the oak tree down the block where the dog was barking. Or nowhere. He could have done the damage, then gone off to gloat. Even with Shane nearby, with my home and family just yards away, I felt exposed and vulnerable. Michael was out to get us, and no one seemed to be able to stop his need for doing harm.

In the light of the street lamp I saw the rose on the ground where Shane had tossed it. I lifted my skirt so as not to let it drag on the ground, and picked up the flower. Wire was entwined in its long stem and the thorns had been removed. The bud was dark colored and limp, as if it had been out of water for a long time. The color seemed darker than the deep red of an American Beauty. I carried the rose closer to the light and held it up. My heart stopped. The rose wasn't deep red at all!

It was *black*! As if it had been dipped in ink.

"Shane!" I cried at the same moment that I heard a strange popping sound, and then another, like stones hitting the car. "Shane!" I ran to where he squatted, tire iron in hand, prying the hubcap off the rear wheel. He looked up. "What?"

"Something hit the car. Didn't you hear . . . ?"

Shane bolted upright and looked around. "What's going—" Before he could say more the popping sound came again, and with it a red flash from the hedges across the street. *"Ow!"* He grimaced, dropped the tire iron, and grabbed his left arm. "Ow!" Blood spurted down the white shirt sleeve.

"You're bleeding!" I cried, scrambling to his side. "What is it?"

"Get down!" he ordered, pulling me with him. "Someone's shooting at us!" He thrust me behind him so I was jammed against the rear fender, protected by his body. Shane's blood made a wet stickiness on my arm. My heart climbed into my throat. Shane reached behind with his right hand and opened the rear car door.

There were two more loud pops and suddenly Michael started shouting, "I told you you'd never make it to the prom! I told you! It's me or nobody, Nicole!"

"Get in the car!" Shane ordered. "Hurry. I'll block you."

I slithered along the fender until I felt the edge of the doorframe against my spine, turned, and dropped to my knees onto the floor inside. I crawled in, catching a heel in my dress, and lay on the floor, nose pressed against the old carpeting.

"How'd you like the balloons, Nicole? Read the message?" Michael shouted.

Oh God. The balloons! In the rush to be ready I hadn't even looked for a card! I should have known by Shane's reaction! "Shane!" I called, urgently. "Get in, quick!"

"I've got to get help!"

"No! Get in!" I squirmed around, and tugged at his pants. "Please! He'll kill you!" I scooted away so there was room for him to climb in next to me. He pulled the door shut behind him.

We huddled on the floor, heads low. Shane gripped his left arm and through clenched teeth said, "Listen.

I counted five shots. If it's a thirty-eight, he's got one more before he reloads."

"Maybe someone heard the shots!" I pictured my own family, probably in the back of the house with the TV on.

"Maybe. I saw lights go on across the street. Damn, this hurts!"

I pulled off my sash. "Lean closer. I'll tie this around the arm. Maybe it'll stop the bleeding."

"No time. Listen carefully, Nicole! We're sitting ducks in here. I think he's after *me*, not you, but who knows? Slip off your heels, open the door on your side, and run! He shouldn't be able to see you with the car blocking his view."

What if he's already crossing the street? I thought, aware of the silence since the last shot. "What about you?"

"I'll be right behind you."

"Maybe I can reason with him!"

"You can't, Nicole! Now don't argue! Open the door and go! Stay in the shadows and make for the backyard."

"I'm scared!"

"Me too! Now, go!"

I pulled off my pumps, reached up and opened the door next to the curb. Crouching as low as possible I scurried out of the car. With my dress held high, I sprinted at top speed up the lawn, aiming for the shade of the tree and the gate to the backyard. I realized my beautiful white dress made such a good target! Every second I expected to feel the sting of a bullet in my back.

Suddenly and shockingly, the car horn blared, went silent, then blared again without stop. Shane was still in the car!

Trembling and out of breath, I reached the wooden gate to the yard. "Help! Help!" I screamed, knowing that my voice gave away my position. On tiptoe I stretched over the gate and groped for the latch. Just as I felt it under my fingers my eyes caught a blur of movement and an arm clamped around my neck, yanking me back.

Choking, I struggled with both hands to free myself. "Help! Let go! Help!" I gasped.

"I knew you'd make a run for it! Take it easy, and I won't hurt you," Michael warned. He swung me around so I formed a shield in front of him. In a quick glimpse I saw he was dressed in army fatigues and combat boots. One arm encircled my neck. The other held a gun straight out, aimed at Shane.

Shane, only steps away, stopped in his tracks. "Leave her alone, Michael! Let her go. It's me you want!" He put his hands up to show surrender.

"Got you good, didn't I?" Michael gloated. "Shoulda done it months ago, taking my girl, turning her against me!"

Above the noise of the car horn I heard sirens far off. For us? "Michael . . ." I huffed. "The police . . ."

His grip tightened. I could hardly breathe. I noticed a neighbor across the way come out of his house, but then he ran back inside.

"Please, *please*, Michael!" I cried. "Let go! You're choking me!"

"Don't cry, you hear me? Stop that! I can't stand it!" Michael hissed. "I wont hurt you, I won't!" I sensed hesitation. Suddenly, he let go and shoved me away. I staggered and fell to my knees.

"Stay away, Shane!" Michael screamed. "I'm warning you!" He reached down with his free hand and touched my shoulder. "Nicole! Are you okay? Nicole, I didn't mean to hurt you!"

I bent over, hugging myself, one hand at my throat, crying and coughing.

"What have I done? What have I done?" Michael seemed crazed with regret. "Help her, Shane! Help Nicole. I don't care! Just get over to her. I'm dead anyway!"

I looked up. Waving the gun, he ran back to the street. Sirens screamed louder now, and I saw cars heading down our street.

Shane rushed to my side and helped me to my feet. "Let's go. Hurry! Come on!" Running, stumbling, we made for the backyard gate, yanked it open, and without looking back, fled inside.

CHAPTER
18

I BANGED ON the back sliding door. In a moment Dad's face appeared. As soon as he saw us he pulled back the drapes and unlocked the door. We rushed inside.

"What's wrong? Shane! You're bleeding! What happened?"

Mom came into the room. "Nicole! Your dress!"

"Michael! He's out there with a gun!"

"He's still got a bullet left!" Shane said. His face looked gray. He squeezed the arm above the wound. "Geez, I'm getting blood all over the place!"

"Help him! Mom! Dad!" Then I rushed to the phone and dialed Michael's number. It seemed forever before a sleepy voice answered. It sounded like Michael's brother. "It's Nicole. Tell your parents Michael's at my house with a gun! I think he may kill himself!"

I hung up without waiting for his brother's response. I raced back to the kitchen where Mom was applying a tourniquet to Shane's arm. Through the breakfast nook window I saw the revolving lights of four police cars. In the middle of the road, spotlighted like a criminal, stood Michael. He held a gun to his head. "Don't Michael! Don't! Oh, please don't!" I begged, though he couldn't hear me.

"What's happening?" Holding one hand to the tourniquet, Shane ran to my side.

"I don't know. I can't hear. I can't see clearly. Maybe the police are talking to him. Oh, Shane! What if he shoots himself! Or they shoot him! It'll be my fault!"

"It will *not* be your fault!" Dad turned off the kitchen light. "Both of you—away from that window! Melanie! Don't you dare open that door!"

A loud voice rang through the house from outdoors, sounding strangely alien. "This is the police! Do not leave your homes. Stay away from windows. Repeat: stay indoors!"

Dad put an arm around my waist. "Come on, honey. Inside."

We went back to the family room, but I couldn't sit. I paced back and forth, picturing Michael outside, police all around him. He said he was "dead anyway." Is that what he meant?

The phone rang suddenly and we all jumped. Dad picked up the receiver. He listened for a moment, then held it out to me. "The police want to talk to you."

"This is Officer Purcel," a woman's voice said. "Is this Nicole Webber?"

"Yes," I said, heart pounding, mouth dry.

"We've got this situation here. Young man with a gun, threatening to shoot himself. Wants to talk with you."

"What should I say?"

"Anything. Just keep him talking. Longer he talks, better chance we have of calming him and getting the gun."

I could hear Michael shouting in the background. He was telling the police to go away, that it was none of their business what he did to himself.

I heard a voice answering. "Be patient. We're trying to reach your girlfriend, like you asked."

"Tell her—tell her—if she won't talk to me it's okay. I understand. Tell her—good-bye!"

"I'll talk to him!" I told Officer Purcel.

"Michael!" I heard the officer call out. "Why don't you put down that gun and come to the phone. Your girlfriend wants to talk to you."

"No! I won't! You're trying to trick me!"

"I'm here, Michael. What do you want?" I had to speak up. The officer said they could amplify my voice so Michael could hear. I didn't even think about what the neighbors would think.

"Nicole!" Michael bellowed, like a wounded animal.

"It's okay, Michael. Do what the officer said and come inside. I'll make hot chocolate, like I used to, and we can talk for as long as you want to. Please, Michael, please."

"Oh, sure. You said you didn't want to have anything to do with me! It's too late. It's over. We both know it."

"Please, Michael. Put down the gun. It'll be all right." My throat knotted so I could hardly speak. "Michael, listen to me. Don't hurt yourself. I couldn't bare it. You have so much to live for!"

"I know the score, Nicole. It's okay. I forgive you. Don't blame yourself. I just want you to know something. I love you. Always have. Just remember that. You're the best thing that ever happened to me. . . ."

He sounded so final. My pulse began to race and I started to cry.

"Oh, man! He's gonna do it! He's got it pointed at his temple," Office Purcel exclaimed.

"Michael!" I shouted. "Wait! Your mother's on her way. She wants to talk to you! You know how she loves you. Your father too. He's coming too."

"He can go to hell."

"Keep talking," Purcel urged. "Say anything, but keep talking."

"Remember the afternoon we went to the zoo, Michael?" I rushed on to say. "In the nocturnal animal house?" I knew Michael would remember; we'd been the only ones there, and it was the first time we'd kissed. I turned my back to Shane, embarrassed that he had to hear.

Michael didn't answer.

"Remember how you tried to teach me to play golf? How we laughed every time I swung the club and tore up the turf?"

Michael still didn't answer. Had he lowered the gun?

I squeezed my eyes shut and searched my memory for other happy times to remind him of and to gain some time.

"Michael!" Purcel's voice rang out. "Your father's here. Nicole," the officer added on the phone to me, "stay with us. We may need you."

"Put that gun down, son!" In the background I heard Mr. Donaldson's booming voice. "Come on, Michael. Give it to me." I pictured him walking slowly forward into the brightly lit road, hand held out to Michael.

"Stay back! Stay back! Come closer and I'll *shoot*!" Michael screamed.

"Okay! Okay! Stay cool!" Mr. Donaldson must have stopped advancing. His voice sounded tired and a little trembly. "Let's go home, Michael. Your mother's worried sick. We'll work out whatever's bothering you, I promise. It'll be all right. We love you, son. Please, just put that gun down!"

"It won't be all right—I killed Shane!"

"No! No, Michael, you didn't!" I cried out. "He's going to be okay. I'll put him on to talk to you if you want!" I gripped the phone and turned to look for Shane. He was staring at me, face pale and tense.

The news must have offered some relief to Michael. I heard the officer say slowly, "That's right. Good boy. Lay it on the ground now, son, that's just fine. Now raise your hands over your head and come forward. Slowly. That's right. Good."

"We've got him. . . ."

From the confusion of police noises and voices, I

made out Mr. Donaldson saying, "It's going to be all right, son. We'll get help. You're gonna be fine."

"It's over, Nicole. We've got him," Purcel said.

"Thank God," I whispered. "Thank God!"

"We've got an ambulance on the way for the injured boy in the house. If he wants to press charges, tell him to come down to the station when he's able."

I dropped the phone into its cradle and slumped against the wall totally exhausted. It was over at last. I didn't have to be afraid anymore. I didn't have to worry about Michael or what he might do to me. The relief made me lightheaded.

Shane came to my side and Mom and Dad and Melanie crowded around.

"They're sending an ambulance, Shane," I said. "They want to know if you'll press charges."

"All I need's a good doctor with a needle and thread and some antiseptic," Shane said. "As for charges, Michael's got enough trouble without my help. I actually feel sorry for the guy."

"Does it hurt much?" Blood seeped through the bandage Mom had wound tightly over his wound. "Where's that ambulance?"

"We'll take him. I'll get my keys," Mom said, leaving the room. "Meet me in the garage."

"What's gonna happen to Michael?" Melanie asked, running after us as we hurried through the kitchen to the garage. "Will Michael be sent to jail?"

"He'll get the psychological help he's needed for a long time," Dad said. "I can't believe it came down to a night like this."

I heard the siren of an ambulance approaching. I stopped in our driveway. In a moment two men pulling a gurney appeared.

Shane winced as they strapped him down, jarring his arm. He gave me a sad smile. "Some prom night, huh? Something we'll never forget."

"Great story material," I tried to joke. My eyes took in his pale face and the blood-stained shirt and pants, and I bent to kiss him. My hair tumbled out of its white ribbon and fell across my face. The ambulance crew rolled him down the drive. I ran along beside him until they lifted the gurney into the ambulance. "I'll call your parents right now. See you in emergency, Texas!" My voice cracked.

I watched until the ambulence backed into the street, its siren blaring, then went inside. Shane would be all right, but what about Michael?

I felt so sad for him, but not guilty. Why should I? I'd tried, really tried to be kind and fair and a good friend. Could I help it if I couldn't love him back?

What a night. All the wonderful plans we had and it came to this. Shane was right. We'd never forget this night. Not ever in our whole lives.

ABOUT THE AUTHOR

GLORIA D. MIKLOWITZ lives in La Canada, California, and speaks frequently at schools and conferences about her work. Some of her other titles include *Anything to Win, Goodbye Tomorrow, Close to the Edge, The War Between the Classes, The Day the Senior Class Got Married, Love Story, Take Three,* and the Starfire novel *Suddenly Super Rich.*